Halibut on the Moon

ALSO BY DAVID VANN

Fiction

Bright Air Black

Aquarium

Goat Mountain

Dirt

Caribou Island

Legend of a Suicide

Nonfiction

Last Day on Earth: A Portrait of the NIU School Shooter

A Mile Down: The True Story of a Disastrous Career at Sea

DAVID VANN

Halibut on the Moon

Grove Press
New York

FIRST EDITION

Published simultaneously in Canada
Printed in the Canada

First Grove Atlantic hardcover edition: March 2019

Library of Congress Cataloging-in-Publication data
is available for this title.

ISBN 978-0-8021-2893-5
eISBN 978-0-8021-4680-9

Grove Press
an imprint of Grove Atlantic
154 West 14th Street
New York, NY 10011

Distributed by Publishers Group West

groveatlantic.com

19 20 21   10 9 8 7 6 5 4 3 2 1

For my stepmother, Nettie Rose.

Halibut on the Moon

The plane descends but there is no San Francisco to see, only cloud and rain in close over the wing, rain at hundreds of miles an hour a horizontal thing only, without fall, without anything light enough to fall. A terrific pressure, insistent, panicked, disappearing and reappearing and come from some terrible source, breath of a god in anger.

Jim waits and hopes, but for what?

Turbulence seems to be the plane's own movement, seems to come from inside, the wing trying to shake something off, but it's a movement in the most enormous river, an irresistible current. The skin will rip, aluminum peel back.

And then waves appear below, whitecaps, scum foam in water muddy brown. All in thin lines, ordered, not the waves of oceans but forced by wind generated right here, newborn waves only minutes old and grown already to full height and breaking and flung a quarter mile from the shore where they began. Our movement is in one direction only, and never a return.

Jim cinches his seat belt for landing, but why? Yellow buoys, rocks of a breakwater. The strip appears below, grass to the side, and they touch down and loft again, a moment of refusal that suspends and might extend forever, but then they touch and their full weight slams forward, engines blown back, brakes gripping, and all is slowed and all pattern of air broken and rain falls downward again.

His brother will be waiting. Gary. Younger brother, now his brother's keeper. Jim become something fragile.

A man in yellow rain slicker waves lit batons to guide. No one around him, endless expanse of pavement.

Final brakes at the gate, and in the moment of surge forward, the last momentum, all rise as one, impelled from their seats, except Jim. He's missed some signal. He would be willing to stay right here for a while longer. He has no idea what to say to Gary, and he knows Gary will have no idea either. Here to escort his older brother to the therapist. The therapist has warned that Jim should not be left alone.

When the others have gone, he rises and takes his valise from the overhead. Brown leather, heavy, holding his pistol, a Ruger .44 magnum, the one Dirty Harry used. Legal to bring on board as long as the shells are in his checked baggage. Separate his guns and shells. More advice from the therapist.

He's the last one to emerge, and Gary the only one left waiting at the gate, standing on thin gray carpet. A nod of recognition, some relief. One stage passed, his brother safely delivered from Alaska. Everyone agrees Alaska isn't good for Jim and never has been. Especially this winter, living alone in a new house on a ridge far from neighbors, living in darkness at the edge of the arctic.

"Red-eye?" Gary asks, their way of saying ready, from hunting, as if they're heading out now at dawn for the lower glades, one driving and the other standing in back of the pickup holding a rifle. Gary looks nervous and so young, thirty-three, six years younger than Jim. But bigger, and Jim can never get used to this. Gary was always the shrimp, shorter than everyone in his year, fast enough still to be on the basketball team, but tiny and thin, and then at Chico, in college, he grew. Most delayed growth spurt anyone had ever heard of, and now he's over six feet and broad shouldered, thick chest from chopping wood and building his own house and coaching basketball at the junior high.

"Ready as I'll ever be," Jim says.

They walk in silence to baggage claim, the aisles almost empty. When they arrive, the bags are out and people loading carts, a lot of coolers taped shut and frozen-goods boxes, everyone bringing back halibut at this time of year, mid-March, no salmon. A connecting flight through Seattle, but still, many of these people were with him in Anchorage. He wasn't aware so many Alaskans had Californian family. He began in Fairbanks, a small plane, ten or so on board. Only thirty thousand people in Fairbanks, Alaska's second-biggest city. Outpost in darkness and cold so far from anything. Every light shining straight up into the heavens because of the ice fog, looking as if all has been beamed from above.

He grabs his green duffel, army surplus, slack, filled to less than a third. The only one not to have packed his bag fully, and what does that mean? Does he need to be more attached to his things and carry more with him? Will that help? He has his shells now, a box of them, within maybe a foot of the magnum. He should be less attached to the pistol and think less about it. He knows that much.

"What's wrong?" Gary asks as they walk through an underground tunnel to the garage.

"What?"

"You're wincing."

"I am?"

3

"Are you in pain?"

"Yeah, I guess so." He becomes more aware of it, the spiral that extends upward from his right eye, track of pain. "The sinus headache, almost always there, worse after a flight."

"You can't have surgery, get some relief?"

Jim is a dentist, so he knows exactly how brutal the surgery would be, the risks, knows the surgeon will be goofing off after Jim is under, making jokes as he cuts away parts of the inside of Jim's head, close enough to the optic nerve to cause blindness, close enough to the brain wall to puncture through.

"You can't just tough it out. You need to come at this thing from all directions, and stopping the physical pain is part of that."

Jim stops walking and looks at his brother. Handsome face, so much more handsome than Jim, who has receding hair and a weak jaw, slack cheeks, caves around his eyes from the insomnia. Gary has none of these. And no wrinkles, only new skin, healthy, eyes clear, hair wavy and blond, long, almost to his shoulders. Still single and always with a different girl-friend, though the current one, Mary, has lasted for a while, so who knows. But Jim envies his younger brother, not only his youth and looks and the women but also his simplicity. He just never stressed out about anything. Felt free to have some beers and hang out with friends and not worry about money or school or family or work. Jim never drank, never could just hang out, worried always about everything, worked his way through high school and college at Safeway, went to church, married the second woman he dated, divorced, married again after almost no dating, divorced again. What made Jim this way and Gary different?

"You look good," Jim says. "Happy and healthy."

"Thanks," Gary says. "But this is about you today."

"Maybe it would help if it weren't about me."

They're really looking at each other now, longest eye contact of their lives, probably. All very strange, and strangely empty. Jim feels nothing as he looks into his brother's eyes, except that this is odd. Blue eyes with hints of yellow or gold. Golden boy Gary. He can feel himself about to laugh.

"Okay," Gary says, and looks away. They walk again.

Euphoria, that's what Jim keeps feeling, several times a day. He can feel it building now, a protective coating from inside. Groundless, without direction, like sitting in soup. Why does anyone think they can control what they feel?

"I've looked up to you all my life," Gary says as they walk. "I need my older brother back. You have to pull it together."

Jim laughs, a low chuckle, genuine. It sounds real. It feels real. "I'm here," Jim says. "It's all going to be okay."

It's a long way to Gary's pickup. An old one, rust brown. "You should get a new truck," he says.

"It's only twelve years old. A sixty-eight. It still runs."

"But barely, right? It's a Dodge. I should know. My Suburban breaks down every other week. Chevy is the same as Dodge, right?"

"What? They're not the same."

Jim has to jam his stuff between them on the bench seat because of the rain. And he thinks what Gary has said is funny. You'd better pull it together. Making threats, because that will certainly help.

They pull onto Highway 101 going north, driving along the water. The waves white and breaking but so tame. No fetch here to build, and the water shallow everywhere along the edges. He and Gary commercial fished for a year on a boat Jim had built, sixty-three-foot aluminum. His dream of escaping dentistry.

"Nothing compared to what we saw, huh?" he says. "The waves."

"Yeah. We saw some waves alright."

"I thought we were going down that time in the straits."

"Yeah. I thought so too. That looked pretty bad."

They were long-lining for halibut in the straits between the Aleutians, at the edge of the Bering Sea, and the line caught on the bottom. The problem was that the seas were thirty feet and breaking, and this line was pinning them down in sick ways. Whenever a wave rose beneath, they were pulled down into it, pressurizing.

"You know, it's a bit like that," Jim says. "The depression, the low points. It's like how our boat was held back and as everything around rises it only pressurizes. It's something like that. Not a perfect description, but something you've felt anyway. Do you remember that?"

"I remember. A feeling inside isn't like that, though."

"Oh, it's much worse. Much stronger. A thirty-foot wave is nothing. A few tens of thousands of pounds of aluminum held down through a wave is something light by comparison."

"That's the problem, the self-pity. You have to get over that. Self-pity is an endless path down."

"There is an end."

"Don't talk about that."

"Isn't that what I'm supposed to do, talk about it?"

Gary drives, both hands on the wheel. The rain blown in white gusts across the road, cars kicking up spray everywhere. The ocean disappearing and appearing again, red taillights showing even in daylight it's so dark.

"I want to talk," Jim says. "I feel like it now. I feel pretty good. I've been in that house alone for too long, just talking with Rhoda on the phone, no one else."

"I called."

"Yeah, a few calls from you and others, but nothing to fill a day. The longer ones have been with her. She helps me plan my day, how I'm going to get through it, step by step."

"She's poison. You need to stay away from her."

"I'm the one who screwed up."

"She's bad news."

"Ah, Rhoda, Rhoda, Rhoda. What is she? You all liked her well enough at our wedding."

"It's not complicated. She's just bad news."

"But it is complicated. She can take a hundred forms. She's every fish in the sea at once."

"Don't do the crazy talk."

"But I am a bit crazy, right? If I'm thinking about suicide and I need a therapist and I need you to escort me? If I drive, I might just yank the wheel into oncoming traffic, or take Highway One and fly off a cliff. So I might as well enjoy the freedom. Because if everyone thinks I'm crazy, I can say anything. And I'm telling you Rhoda is not what any of you imagine. She's better and more. She's tougher than any of us. Her mother just blew a hole in her husband with a shotgun, right in their living room as he's trying to run away. Shot him in the back from maybe ten feet and then offs herself with a pistol. No hesitation."

"It's probably not good for you to think too much about that."

"But it is. There's not some safe place I can go. You and Mom and Dad think there's a safe place."

"Well staying away from her would be a start. And visiting us."

"You're all more dangerous than she is."

"Stop that."

"This is why you're more dangerous. Because you're not honest. She's honest, and far tougher. Less than a year ago she loses her parents like that, and here she is now, talking me through my day, helping me make a plan, even though nothing happened in my life. Where's my great tragedy to blame for being so fucked up now?"

They're on the city streets. Some idiot designed 101 to pass the longest possible way, through about fifty traffic lights.

"I'd like to see a prostitute," Jim says.

"You don't want to do that, at least not here."

"You used to go to Nevada, right?"

"Yeah, but that's different, and it's legal, an entire old-time town built for it, with plank sidewalks and dirt streets. They make it look real. Saloons and hoop dresses and whiskey in old bottles. They even changed the bottles."

"I want to go. I need to see that before I die, so we need to go this trip."

"Don't talk like that."

"I'm supposed to talk. Everyone wants me to talk, and then they don't want me to talk. I'm telling my brother I want him to take me to that Wild West town where I wear my six-gun and do a bunch of whores. I want to feel free. I never did anything. And who cares now if I catch something to make my dick fall off. It doesn't matter."

Gary isn't responding. Just white-knuckling the wheel and staring at the car ahead, stop and go, stop and go.

"It would be so easy," Jim says. "It would be just so easy, at any moment, and think how long a day is, how many moments in every single day, and the nights even longer. No one around at night. Only me."

"Please," Gary says, his voice really pleading, desperate. "Please try. I know you can get back to your old self."

"I'm sorry," Jim says. "I'm not trying to hurt you. But there is no old self. There's nothing to go back to. That's what people don't understand. There's no self at all. There's no one home."

A kind of groan then from Gary, a sound of despair, nameless.

"I'm sorry," Jim says, but Gary seems incapable of responding now. So strange. In his time of need, Jim will have to take care of everyone in his family. He will need to reassure, but what would any reassurance be but denial? Only Rhoda will be frank with him. The hard truth, something she's always liked, and something he's always been afraid of, though when you're far enough gone, the fear goes away too. Fear is only when there's something to save.

"I've been thinking about Mom and Dad," Jim says. "I know you don't want me to talk right now, but I'm going to talk anyway. I've been thinking I have this core feeling that I'm a piece of shit, that I'm not good enough, and I wonder where that came from. It must be them. I can't have been born with it. I'm thinking it must be from Mom's religion more than anything else, from telling me even now I have to have god. Because the problem is I don't have god. So what am I supposed to do then?"

"You're almost forty years old. Just don't go to church. Don't blame them."

"I don't go to church, but that's the problem. Inside I know I'm good only if I do go and I do believe."

"That's your problem. Don't blame them."

"Why are you protecting them? Are they suicidal? Do they need to be treated carefully right now?"

"Well what does Dad have to do with it?"

"He just expected me to work, because he was expected to work, and he expected me to be a dentist like him, but he knows I'm nothing just like he's nothing."

"You're not nothing. You have a ridiculous amount of money. I'm a teacher. I can tell you about nothing."

"But you wanted to be a teacher. That's the difference. I didn't want to be a dentist, and neither did Dad."

"Well then change. Do something else."

"There's this weird thing about dignity. I did the commercial fishing because I love boats and fishing. That was a dream. But when it didn't work out, all I could do was go back to dentistry, because everything else lacked dignity. I'd be taking a big step down. I can't do that."

"Nobody's putting a gun to your head."

"Well except myself."

Gary doesn't respond to that one. Crossing the Golden Gate now, narrow lanes and water thrown by trucks to cover the windshield, all blind and then seen again, red steel and red lights and all submerged.

"I've been thinking about our heritage," Jim says. "That there was a chief in my name, Jim Vann, and one in my son's name, David Vann, and even Dad's name goes back. There are other Roys, though they used the full name, Royal. And it's not just the Cherokee chiefs, but also further back the Vanes with Raby Castle in England and one of them accepting the surrender of a French king, given a golden gauntlet, and Henry Vane, I think it was, who was the governor of Massachusetts, also, when it was a colony, and helped found Harvard but later was beheaded when he returned to England, and we have a famous pirate, also, Charles Vane, and medieval knights and we're even related to Roy Rogers. I grew up thinking we were nothing, that we came only from farmers, because Dad never said anything, and then I find out we have these higher origins, and I wonder if there's something in me that knows we've failed, that we've gone too low now, and will never be satisfied."

"That's ridiculous."

"Can you say how your mind has been made? Can you say where your thinking comes from or where your personality comes from, why you are certain ways and not others?"

"I don't have to say. I just am."

"That's great, honestly. That is the perfect and healthy thing anyone would want to be. I wish I could be that. I'm happy for you, and I want you to keep that. Even if something happens to me, you have to keep that, because it's worth more than anything else in this world."

Sausalito and Marin, San Rafael and half a dozen other towns in the sprawl north of the gate, all rich but dumpy looking. Empty places, but every place empty now to Jim. He realizes he's not seeing clearly. Encased in rain and spray and low cloud, but that's only the minor distortion.

"Everything does look different," Jim says. "I thought I was feeling the euphoria, that it would last for a while, at least until we got to Santa Rosa, but it's gone already and I do see every house, every building as depressing and small and unbearable, and all of California closed in, and the sky too low. It really is like that, as if everything is moving toward me but will never reach me."

"You might be okay, actually, talking so much about what you see and how you feel. That's supposed to be a good sign, right? I was warned about when you're not talking."

"Yeah, I think you're right. Maybe something has shifted. I don't know."

"Well we'll find out soon enough. We'll be at the therapist in another half hour or forty minutes."

"The therapist doesn't offer much. If he were there in my final moments, he'd write down some notes about how I'm holding the gun. Why is it you close one eye when you hold the barrel to the side of your head? What does that mean? Have you always felt unsafe? When did it begin? When did you first close that eye?"

"Stop!" Gary yells.

Jim is surprised by the volume, by the suddenness of it. "Fuck, okay. Sorry, little brother."

So Jim tries to be a good citizen: just sit on his end of the bench seat and not say anything, not even think anything, not wonder about source or meaning. Impossible anyway to say how the thoughts began, how despair began, how he ended up here now. He watches the landscape open, green hills and fields dotted with large oaks, oak savannah it's called, though artificially cleared. Who knows what it looked like hundreds of years ago, whether this was an open valley or filled with trees. All green at the moment, the prettiest time in California, before it all turns brown.

The Cherokee woman his ancestor married, what about her parents or grandparents? One of those generations would have reached back to the Stone Age, to hunter-gatherers, so recent here, a pocket in time. Other side of the country, on the East Coast, in Virginia, but the same life, fishing and hunting, gathering native plants. No therapists, no cars or roads, rituals for each stage in life and always belonging. Would he have been suicidal then, or is it only in this time and culture that his equation turns out that way? Can you think about suicide when you have to think every day about finding food?

Jim would like to go back, has always wanted to go back. He loves hunting and fishing, and there was a time when all was plentiful. Even just seeing what happened to Alaska in the seventies is an unspeakable loss, all the big halibut gone from Southeast in only a decade, and the salmon will be next. He doesn't want any of the stuff of modern life, only everyone gone and the land rich again, and he'll go back two hundred years or five hundred years, as long as it takes.

Dr. Brown, the therapist, has encouraged him to think of what his freer life might be. What if he didn't have to be a dentist, what if he didn't have to need Rhoda and could let her go, what if he decided to just not worry about the $365,000 he owes the IRS, a thousand for every day of the year? That's a debt that will never leave, but he could leave. His passport still works. The IRS hasn't prohibited him from leaving the country. So what if he just drove to Mexico or flew to Asia or Africa, somewhere he could live cheap, drawing all his cash first before he goes? It's possible. It is possible. But he sees himself alone in a room somewhere, always alone. He doesn't know how leaving becomes a life, how it becomes filled with other people. Aren't the people we have already the only people we will have? Isn't our family what makes us, forever, and the woman we love?

"I couldn't leave my children," he says, and then realizes he's spoken aloud.

"What?" Gary asks.

"Sorry."

"What do you mean by leaving your children?"

"Something Dr. Brown said, that I could just leave, go to Guatemala or Africa and never come back, change my life, but I'd have to come back to see David and Tracy. I couldn't just leave them forever. And you, Mom, Dad, Ginny, Rhoda. I can't just leave."

"Well yeah. You need us to help you through this. We're the ones who love you. You have to let your family help you."

"I guess his point was that family might be what's killing me. And my job and all the stuff of my current life. Not that it's your fault, but just the way things are. Maybe getting away is my only chance."

"He can't be saying that."

"But he is."

"He can't recommend you leave us."

"A therapist is not out to preserve anything. Most people don't know that. They're only trying to free the individual. In some ways, suicide fits with what they do. He wants to free me from everything that's causing pressure, including everything inside, so he should let me just do it. All pain and suffering gone, forever."

"If he ever recommends suicide, you tell me, and I'll strangle him myself."

"He's not going to recommend it. But he is willing to recommend leaving any social bond or job, leaving family and all responsibility. Like throwing all the heavy shit off the boat when it's sinking."

"The boat still sinks, because there's a hole in it some-where. They don't sink from being too heavy, unless you're talking top-heavy and rolling."

"True."

"I think you're thinking more of airplanes, having to jet-tison cargo when the fuel is running low."

"It was just a metaphor."

"Well."

And then he's thinking of Rhoda, just like that, his brother a distraction for maybe forty minutes before she's taken over again. He wants to see her, right away. He's thinking of her from behind, buried all the way in and grabbing a fistful of her hair, and he has a boner already. He jacks off maybe five times a day now, even though he's been warned that sexual exhaustion is part of the end, part of how the end is made possible.

He looks out the side window so nothing will show on his face. Can other people tell when we're thinking about sex?

Being here in the truck is unbearable. He feels encased in lead and held down. He has nothing to say to his brother. He just wants to fuck. If it can't be Rhoda tonight, he'll find someone else. She's probably fucking her new man, Rich. Some loser from Konocti with no money who's named Rich, ridiculously, but he has what Jim wants. Some shit bag who never worked hard but happened to be in the right place. No fairness in this world, no reward for doing things right, and certainly no reward for being smarter. Thoughts are only a curse. He wants his brother's brain, thinking nothing while drinking a can of beer, feeling oddly happy for no reason at all and not wondering about that, not a single reflection on his own existence.

"You're moaning," Gary says. "Or groaning or something. Some low sound. Are you even aware you're doing that?"

Jim turns forward, stares out the windshield. So much for hiding. "No. I wasn't aware."

"Is that happening more, that you don't realize what you look like and sound like?"

"How would I know? Just think about your question."

"Well have other people noticed?"

"What other people? I'm alone up there, remember? There's no furniture, even. Just a folding card table and two folding chairs. I haven't been going into work. I can moan all day and no one will notice."

"You can't go back there."

"It's where I live. It's my new house. I just had it built."

"Just leave it."

"Momentum. That's the most important word in our lives. We have to follow momentum, even if we know what's coming isn't good. You can't fight it. Like trying to swim upriver. If you struggle, you're faced the wrong way and see even less of what's coming."

"That's the biggest load of shit you've said so far."

"Is it?"

"There's no river. And this isn't you. You have to come back to who you are."

"But this is me."

"I know my brother. I've known him all my life, from my earliest memories, and I know he laughs and makes jokes and has fun and likes to hunt and fish and doesn't let pressures get him down. But he went to college and met Elizabeth and started to feel some pressure, about getting married and providing for his family, and it was dental school, also, when you were in San Francisco. Something happened in those couple of years. And then you had to serve in the navy up on Adak and that pushed you a bit further. Then you had a son, and I think you were happy about that, but then you cheated on your wife and broke up your family as your daughter was born, and that put you lower, feeling guilty, and then you met Rhoda, and she was the worst. She brought you down far lower than the rest of it. So there's no mystery about what happened, or when, and there's no momentum. There's only bad choices, and you can stop making those choices. Don't go to Alaska, and don't ever see Rhoda again. Come back to California and live with me and return to school to get your certificate and become a teacher if that's what you want. See your family more. You need to be with us, and then you'll be fine. See your kids more too. Where I live in Sebastopol is only twenty minutes away from them. You could see them all the time."

"What is it that's so bad about Rhoda?"

"It's what she does to you. She makes you so unhappy. I don't know how she does it."

"She makes me see who I am."

"That's not you, only you around Rhoda."

"I've been up there three months and haven't seen any of you, including her. So this is the me when I'm around me."

Gary doesn't respond to that, so Jim looks out his window again. Fields, mostly, in the area south of Santa Rosa. Farm country. Petaluma a small town, really. He always thinks of California as too crowded, overrun by people, but it's not true. Plenty of open space still. Not like Alaska, though, where you might hike five hundred miles and never cross a road if you set out in the right direction.

The basis for every decision unfirm. He left California because it was too crowded and the hunting and fishing not good enough anymore, but the fishing is dying in Alaska now too, and if he spends most of his time in Fairbanks, he's living in a town with people just like living in a town with people anywhere else.

Gary believes everything is clear, but nothing is clear, not one of those moments in his history. Jim doesn't know why

he's done anything he's done. All conscious decisions understood later to be something other than conscious.

"This is the truth," he says out loud. "We think we know
what we're doing, and why, but we don't."

"The most important thing you have to remember is that
you're not thinking straight right now. Nothing you're thinking right now is the truth. You're suffering, and everything is
thrown off by that. You're like a compass next to a magnet.
So don't trust any of this. Just trust your family. We'll get
you through."

Dr. Brown may not actually have a PhD. It's unclear. What he does have is an enormous wall of glass that looks out to overgrown forest, trees all moving now in the wind. Jim is staring at the storm in close, and then that idea seems like the perfect metaphor for therapy, so he smiles.

"And what is that smile about?" Dr. Brown asks.

"You have my head in your backyard. That's why you have this big window. You know that no one can look at a forest and not see themselves."

"That's right. It functions as a Rorschach test. Do you know what that is?"

"Yes."

"And what do you see?"

"Isn't that being too obvious?"

"Obvious is okay. We're trying to see together, as clearly as possible."

"A storm in close, that's what I see, everything bending and blown. And when the wind accelerates, nothing is ready for that."

"But it all bends and comes back, right?"

"Yeah."

"Tell me more about the wind."

"It doesn't have a source. And there's no limit to how quickly it can accelerate or what it can become. I know from being on the ocean fishing and seeing what it does. In an hour the entire world can change."

"The ocean is the best Rorschach test, the largest and purest. Our unconscious. What was it like to be out there?"

"It was freedom, and never the same moment twice. The water never looked the same, or the sky. The sky has been taken over by the water too."

"How far out were you?"

"A couple hundred miles a few times. Not as far out as you can go. But anything past about twenty-five miles might be more or less the same. There's no land and no safety."

"And what happened when the wind came?"

"It builds waves more quickly than you would think. It arrives with them already made and they keep increasing, getting steeper, starting to break. But that's not what's terrifying. It should be. It's the real danger. But all you can focus on is the sound of the wind, the way it howls and whines and sings using everything on the boat: the outriggers, which are these long poles with drogues suspended for balance to keep us from rolling side to side so much, and the antennas and railings, all of it becomes tuned and produces noises you wouldn't believe, some of them like ghosts. You wonder what a sound is, and you can't imagine it could come from the boat. It begins to seem to come from outside, from something else that might be near."

"It's not the real danger, but it's where you focus and what you're afraid of."

"Yes."

"And what is that now? What takes all your focus now?"

"Sex. Sex with Rhoda. All the ways I want to fuck her."

"And that's not the real danger?"

"No."

"And what is the real danger now? What are the waves?"

Jim has his eyes closed, remembering the Bering Sea, the size of those waves, thirty feet, like three-story buildings looming above and breaking white, dumping enough weight onto the deck to make the entire boat flex and bounce, then gone. Rising up from all sides. "I don't know if the waves are there or not," Jim finally says. "You can't hear them until they come in close. You can't see them because it's night. The storms always come at night, not only in my life now but also at sea, as if they know they have to be metaphor. We never had a big storm hit during the day, not once. They always waited for the most terrifying time to get us."

"Where do the waves come from?"

"Maybe from everything I've done that's bad, from cheating on my wife and breaking up our family, not being there for my kids. From breaking up my second marriage too. Not only cheating but seeing prostitutes and passing along crabs."

"But waves only last for a short time in the ocean, right? A storm builds them, and they might cross the entire Pacific, thousands of miles, but then eventually they hit shore and are no longer a problem, right, and they probably diminish before that?"

"Yeah, and that's how inside is different and not like the ocean. In here, all waves grow over time, and they circle the entire globe and come back again, like the Southern Ocean actually, and I never know when that will be."

"Is that the most frightening part, that you don't know when they will hit?"

"Yes."

"Is there something you could do to help prepare yourself for the next time they come?"

"I don't know." Jim is staring at the trees, watching them bend, and he knows the force of that will be magnified a million times, that there's no limit.

"Maybe there's something we can say about the waves when they arrive, something to remember about them, a kind of mantra. What is it that you know about the waves now but forget when they arrive?"

"I forget the size of my body."

"What's that?"

"When the waves hit, my body swells. It becomes enormous, under too much pressure. Especially my head. And my hands."

"What words would help you remember their real size?"

"This is not my body."

"Hm. I don't know if I want to use that. Seems too easy to harm your body then. We have to find some other words. What other words can help you remember?"

"I don't know."

"The words have to come from you. Something to remember the real size of your body and to remember that you can be safe again after the waves pass."

"My body will return. It will come back."

"Maybe something more particular than that, something to focus on?"

"I don't know."

"Okay, let's use that then, for now. My body will return. It will come back. Although I don't like that either. Sounds like reincarnation, like it's okay for the body you feel then to go. We can't use that."

"There's nothing that will work anyway. The waves can become anything, and they're inside. There's no escaping them." Jim can feel his pulse hard now, fingers swelling, head beginning to swim.

"You look uncomfortable. What are you feeling now?"

But Jim can't speak. He closes his eyes and sees the tracery of pain in his head and feels the gulf below, something to fall through endlessly as it grows in size and pressure.

"Tell me what you're feeling, Jim."

"It's more like quicksand than waves, more like sinking or falling as it grows around me, and I won't be able to breathe. Everything tightening."

"This is panic, Jim. It's natural. It's okay. When we feel overwhelmed, we panic, and that's our way of surviving. You're a survivor. You're going to get through this. You're doing exactly the right thing. Now I want you to just focus on your breath, on your exhale. Let it out all the way, slowly. Yes. And now again, let your breath out slowly. This is what you'll do whenever this happens, just know that it's all okay and all you have to do is focus on your breath. The panic is your clearest sign that you want to live."

Jim wonders if this is true. Does he want to live?

"I need to ask you some questions, Jim. I'm sorry to do this when you feel uncomfortable, but we have only a short time, so I have to start asking now. Just keep focusing on your exhales, letting your breath go and letting everything be easy."

Letting everything be easy. That's what Jim would like. No longer struggle.

"Have you had thoughts of hurting yourself?"

"Hurting myself? Only suicide, but not hurting myself. I don't want to feel any pain. I'm tired of pain."

"Is it the sinus pain still?"

"Yes, but more than that, some kind of grief about my life, some pain about who I've become and everything I've done and also what's waiting for me, the IRS and all that."

"I'm sorry. There's so much to talk about, but I need to just ask a series of questions now. I'm required to."

"Okay."

"Have you imagined how you might commit suicide? Have you imagined the method?"

"Yes. My pistol."

"Do you have your pistol with you?"

"Yes."

"In this room?"

"No. In the truck, in my bag."

"Have you separated your gun and shells, as I asked?"

"Yes. But not separated far."

"Would you consider giving the pistol to someone now for safekeeping, until you're feeling better?"

"No. I like having it."

"Have you imagined hurting anyone else, shooting anyone else?"

"No."

"Are you sure? What about Rhoda, if you see her and she wants to be with another man and you feel angry?"

"No."

"Even though she lost her parents that way? That doesn't make it possible for you to think about shooting her?"

"No. I would never do that."

"And what about your children, David and Tracy? When you see them, if you feel sad and don't want to leave them, is there any chance you might try to take them with you, kill them first and then kill yourself?"

"No. No."

"Are you angry at them, or at your ex-wife, Elizabeth?"

"No. She's fine. They're fine. I want them to be happy. I would never hurt them."

"Okay."

Dr. Brown pauses a moment and swivels to the side to look at the trees. He's only a few years older than Jim.

"I can't be saved," Jim says. "Thank you for trying, but there are too many hours alone. It just goes on and on and everything hurts. My whole body hurts."

"I'd like you to try some medication. I was trying to avoid that, but you're fighting against so much, the medication will help. It changes your mood. Instead of falling, you'll be on solid ground. You'll be more stabilized."

"How long does it take to work?"

"It takes several weeks."

Jim smiles.

"What's that smile about?"

"Like being on a ship in a storm and someone says help is coming in several weeks."

"Look, Jim." Dr. Brown is leaning forward across his desk now. "You're suffering, but you're a smart man, and you know you have your children to live for and you know there's still so much you can do in life. I don't normally talk like this during therapy. I try not to give my opinion. But you're in a crisis now, and you need to know you can get through this. So I'm telling you I've seen people suffering far more, with less to live for, who pulled through. Sixteen years I've been doing this. What you have to do is give your pistol to someone to keep for you. And you can't be left alone, not for the next couple weeks until the medication stabilizes. I'm going to talk with your brother and make sure he understands that. Okay?"

"Okay."

"Let's go talk with him now, then. And you did good work today, talking about the waves. You're better able to understand and express what's happening than anyone else I've worked with who's feeling this way, so that's an excellent sign."

"The signs are all good. The omens."

"Yes, but I wouldn't use that word."

"Why not?"

"Because of the helplessness, the sense of fate in the Greeks. We're not determined by omens."

"But what if that's all we're doing here, reading signs? What if there's no changing course but only trying to see what's coming?"

"You can always change course. But let's go out now and talk with your brother."

Dr. Brown rises and crosses the room to open the door. He seems self-conscious, awkward in his walk, as if he's worried what Jim will think of his walking, and this makes Jim smile.

Jim pauses at the door, makes a broad sweep of his arm letting himself out, a grand gesture. He likes this thought, a grand gesture of exit. Maybe that's why suicides kill others first, to provide some punctuation, to make it all mean more than nothing. He has, in fact, imagined shooting Rhoda first, on this very trip if he has a chance to meet her, but it's not an abstract thing, an idea of the meaning of it all. It's pure rage and satisfaction. A gun demands to be used. A heavy pistol like a .44 magnum, meant for bears, wants carnage like in *Dirty Harry*. It's in the nature of the thing itself, and it matches something inside Jim, some anger that the world wasn't put together right, that all rules were meant to screw him from the first.

Dr. Brown follows him to the pickup and has made no comment about his gesture at the door. Every small tic examined, but not the grand gestures.

Raining still, and Jim doesn't care. Dr. Brown has an umbrella but Jim strides bareheaded, steps in whatever part of a puddle is in his line. He likes the feeling of the rain, cold but nothing like Alaska. Reassuring to have the sky finally touch, to be able to reach it after all the taunting.

"Well here we are," he says when he reaches the pickup.

Gary has rolled his window down. "Don't just stand there in the rain," he says. "Come around and get in."

"I like it here," Jim says.

Dr. Brown stands close enough to cover him with the umbrella, a disappointment. Wet smell of Brown in close, or is that the smell of Jim's jacket? Wool that he's used on hunts and camping, washed but still holding every campfire and the blood of mountain goats and Dall rams, caribou, deer, salmon, halibut. Reassuring.

"I've prescribed medication for your brother," Dr. Brown tells Gary.

"And what about for *my* brother?" Jim asks. "Any help there?"

They ignore him. Neither even looks at him, but he knows he spoke aloud.

"It will take two weeks to settle, so he can't be left alone during those two weeks. His guns and shells have to be separated, and any other guns where he might be staying, and really someone should be keeping his pistol for him at this time. He shouldn't have it."

So strange to be talked about in this way. And no mention of the danger he might take others with him. What kind of warning doesn't include that?

Gary is nodding as if these are simple directions. How to make a soup, or the turns to find the highway again. And why this sudden belief in the medication? Why didn't he start weeks ago, while he was still reliably alive for several more weeks?

One shoulder still taking rain, getting colder. "Enough of this," he says. "Just give me the medication. You should have given it to me before." He feels angry suddenly, so angry. The short session, overcharged, and standing here in the rain being talked about as if he's a child.

"We'll go back to my office," Brown says. "All three of us, to talk for a few minutes, then I'll give you the prescription."

"And I'll pay."

"Yes."

So the three of them walk back through the rain into the office that pretends to offer no shelter, pretends to be open to the forest. Three men who will huddle around a campfire and try to understand something about what to do next and why, because what meaning has there ever been, from the first time men huddled around fire? All the struggle to survive, for hundreds of thousands of years, every single person struggling, and for what?

Dr. Brown offers him a small towel. "To dry your head," he says, and Jim laughs.

"What?" Brown asks.

"That's perfect. My head's wet. We found the problem."

"Please," Gary says. "Please try here. You're not trying."

"I'm not trying. Says he who's been through the same struggle, felt the same things, been the same person."

Gary is so big and looks so small, helpless.

"Let's sit," Brown says, so they do, Jim and Gary on the couch at opposite ends, slouched low.

"We have a plan," Brown says. "And the purpose of a plan is to make everything easy and clear. It's okay if you feel confused, if you feel angry, if you feel a range of things. That doesn't affect the plan. No matter what you feel, no matter what happens, you just follow the plan. And the plan is this: you don't leave Jim alone, Gary. You or someone else with him at all times, and that includes sleeping in the same room with him at night. Guns away from him, with shells separated. No big knives, no keys to the car. Jim is at the highest risk. He has to be watched. If you want, he can enter a facility right now, a hospital, where he'll be under care and supervision. This is a crisis time. But I can't put him there against his will. It has to be his choice, made freely."

"A nuthouse?" Jim asks. "You'd put me in a nuthouse?"

"That's not what it is. It's a place with professional help and supervision."

"Fuck that. I saw *One Flew Over the Cuckoo's Nest*. No thanks."

"Okay, fine. We'll take that off the table. But Gary, you can't let him be alone. And Jim, you can't go back to Alaska alone. I don't recommend you see Rhoda during this trip, either."

"That's what I've been telling him," Gary says.

"I'm going to see her if I can. She's not the problem."

"It's true she's not the problem. But your desperate feelings about her push you in the wrong direction. It's better to avoid high-stress situations right now. Anything that makes you feel angry."

"We're supposed to feel angry when we've been screwed, right? Isn't that an appropriate feeling?"

"The problem is the swing. You feel euphoric and then you crash into despair and rage, then euphoria again, then completely lost and desolate, right?"

"Yeah, that's actually a pretty good description."

"You feel that?" Gary asks.

"It's why I'm so fun to be around. Such good entertainment value."

"The medication will level things out, keep you from swinging so far in either direction."

"I won't feel the euphoria?"

"No."

"But I like it. Can't someone come up with a drug that kills only the lows?"

"Cocaine," Gary says.

"Let's not talk about recreational drugs," Brown says. "You certainly don't want to add that. And our time is up. I have another appointment. But I'll write the prescription right now and give you a couple samples to start."

31

"So that's it?" Jim asks. "I fly down from Alaska to be saved, and this is it? Medication that will help two weeks from now, and a warning to my brother to watch me as if I'm a child?"

"I think you know we've talked about more than that. You made good progress today in talking about the waves."

"Waves?" Gary asks. "What waves?"

Brown is bent over his prescription pad, scribbling. Happy to be finished with Jim, and wouldn't everyone be happy to be finished with Jim, including Jim? And isn't this Jim smiling at this thought? Nice one, fucker. Laugh yourself to the grave. "Finished with Jim," he says. "We all want to be finished with Jim. Rhoda too. She wants me to leave her alone so she can move on to her new life with Rich, the poor fuck from Konocti. Wants to marry him."

"I'm sorry, but our time is up. We'll have to talk more about Rhoda next time. We're meeting just three days from now, correct? At two p.m.?"

"That's right," Gary says. "I'll bring him back down."

"Don't forget the wet naps," Jim says. "In case I make a doo-doo."

"I'll show you to the door," Brown says, rising. "And that'll be sixty dollars, please."

"Callous fuck," Jim says. "This is my life, right at the end."

"It doesn't have to be," Brown says. "You can get through this, Jim. You have everything to live for still, including your children, and you can make changes in your life. For now, just focus on the next three days."

"That's a world of time. How about one day?"

"Even better."

32

Jim hands him three twenties and takes the prescription and samples. "Fuck you for not giving a shit if I die right now."

Brown takes the money. He's holding the door open and doesn't say anything. He isn't even looking at Jim. Wavy hair, sideburns, probably trying to be a ladies' man, picking up women by analyzing them and offering to fuck them two weeks from now.

"Fine," Jim says and walks out.

"You can't tell your therapist to fuck off," Gary says. "You need him."

"You can fuck off too."

"That's great. You're really trying here."

"If you knew what the middle of the night is like, when I can't sleep, then you'd be a tad disappointed, too, at what's been offered today."

"Let's focus on real things, then. We're going now to see your kids. Think of them when it's the middle of the night. Think of them without a father for the rest of their lives."

Wide streets in Santa Rosa, lots of trees. They climb into small hills, Hidden Valley, go up Oak Hill Drive and the house is on the left. His son, David, playing basketball in a short, curved driveway with a hoop too low. Blond hair, too long, parted down the middle and feathered back, his son looking like a girl, a pink plastic comb in the back pocket of his bell-bottoms, which are too tight.

"We never looked like that," he says.

"It's fine," Gary says. "They all look like that now. My hair is long too."

"Well I don't like it."

They pull into the driveway, and David comes running for Jim's side of the truck, smiling, and that does make Jim grin. There's nothing like how your children love you, no matter who you are or what you've done.

"Dad!" Such a simple thing.

Jim opens his door and his son gives him a hug, then his daughter, Tracy, is there, too, unbelievably cute, only eight years old, wisps of blonde hair held in butterfly barrettes, wearing a pink sweater. She feels so soft and small when he picks her up.

"I made you a present," she says.

"Oh really?" he says. "What's that?"

"Hiya, Jim." It's Elizabeth, his ex-wife, come out to the driveway also, standing a bit farther away. She looks happy and healthy, wide smile. They've gotten along fine in all the years of their divorce, never fighting in front of the children, which is good.

"Well," Jim says, feeling overwhelmed. Tracy is a bit heavy to hold now, so he lets her down.

Then everyone seems to be talking at once. He can't focus. Elizabeth asking how his trip was, his son asking if they can go hunting, his daughter wanting to show him the present, Gary saying something about this evening. It's all too much, and he can't tell what he feels. Like being buried and flying at the same time.

So he stands in the cool air, under clouds massed and gray, heavy but not dumping rain at the moment, and he keeps one hand on the hood of the truck for balance, warm from the drive. He can smell the engine.

What's odd is that his children don't know. They don't realize how far gone he is. All the adults know. Even Elizabeth, whom he hasn't really talked to, is looking at him strangely, understanding something, but David is focused only on hunting, going today, right here in Santa Rosa.

"I don't think there's anywhere to hunt here, sweetie," Elizabeth says, but David is insistent.

"We'll just use the pellet gun," he says. "Just go for quail." Thirteen years old, so young he's not quite real. Hard to believe there's a mind in there working independently. Changing so fast he's a stranger now to Jim. How did the David from three months ago, at Christmas, become this David? There have been changes, and Jim wasn't there. He must have a secret life too. Jacking off all the time, no doubt, just like Jim, but his face looks so innocent and smooth it's hard to believe. Are his thoughts of girls, or hunting, or homework, or friends, or his father, or something else? Jim wouldn't know.

What Jim wanted was for them to have a year together, his son coming up to Fairbanks for the school year, but David said no. So every visit will be this way, with something changed and lost and never made continuous or believable, never known.

"We can do it," Jim says. "Why not. We can drive into the hills and pull off somewhere to hunt for quail."

"It's all private land around here," Gary says. "I don't know if that's such a good idea."

"We'll just do it," Jim says. "Get your pellet gun and make sure you and your sister have your rain jackets and hiking boots."

"Yeah!" David says, excited, and he's running into the house. Tracy is hopping up and down, excited but probably not knowing what's going on.

"Jim," Elizabeth says. "You can say no. This doesn't sound like a good plan."

"It'll be fine. It's only a pellet gun. We won't end up in prison."

"We're planning to have dinner tonight at Mary's," Gary says. "There's a full moon tonight if the sky clears, so we can get out the spotting scope. There's not much light where Mary lives. It's pretty clear."

"When will they be back?" Elizabeth asks.

"How about by nine?" Jim says.

"Okay. And Jim, are you alright? You seem low."

"Yeah," he says, but his chest feels so tight he can't say more than that. Why didn't he stay with her and have his family?

There was a time it seemed impossible to stay. Now he wonders why it was so hard. She loved him and thought all was good, some kind of fairy-tale fantasy he disrupted. He had felt his life closing in too fast, having a second child, a house in Ketchikan, living in a small community and everything known by everyone, and most of all the emptiness, sitting with her at dinner in the evening with nothing to say. Terrifying how slow and empty and small that felt. But still, look what he would have now if he had stayed. A family, his kids old enough to talk to, share things with, probably no emptiness now, their lives too busy for that, if only he had waited.

"What's wrong, Jim?" she asks.

"Just everything," he says. "I'm sorry we're not a family. I'm sorry I wrecked everything."

"Jim, that was a long time ago. You have to forgive yourself for that. You're a good person, a good father."

He realizes Tracy is holding his hands, swinging his arms a bit from below. He kneels down and she collapses against him in a hug that's just pure love.

"I love you, Daddy," she says, as if on cue, as if she knows this is the time to save him, but the truth is she knows nothing and also can do nothing to help him. She's far away. She won't be there each night when he can't sleep, and his thoughts would be unimaginable to her, monstrous. Her daddy so much worse than anything she could imagine from a fairy tale.

"I love you too," he says. "I love you and your brother more than anything." But he wonders about this. It's true he feels an ache whenever he leaves them. It feels wrong every time they say goodbye. And he thinks of them and has some abstract sense that they are most important. But he thinks of

Rhoda more. She's the one he misses late at night and even right now. This may be his last trip seeing his children, and still he can't focus.

He holds one hand on the back of her head. "Tracy," he says. "I hope all of your life is good, that you never feel terrible, that you're never lost." But he realizes what he's going to do to her, what she'll feel when her father is gone so suddenly. And since David is older, he'll feel it more, probably, though who can know?

"Jim," Elizabeth says. "She's eight years old."

"Sorry," he says, and lets Tracy go and stands back up. "I'm not myself really."

Elizabeth steps closer and puts a hand on his back. "It's okay. You're going to get through whatever it is. You have so many people who love you."

Then David is back out with his pellet gun and the rain jackets, smiling. Lopsided grin just like Jim's. "I brought all the pellets," he says. "And my slingshot too." He's carrying a Wrist Rocket, aluminum frame and surgical tubing for the bands, so much more powerful than anything from when Jim was a kid. Steel ball bearings for ammo. "You have to see the crossbow I made."

They all walk through the garage to the backyard. David's crossbow is a piece of wood with another nailed at the end in a T. Thick surgical tubing leading to a pouch of leather. Jim steps closer to examine, and it's pretty good. A long groove for the arrow, a thick nail that acts as the trigger.

"Pretty nifty," Jim says. "Let's see it in action."

David smiles, obviously proud. He has a target arrow with a rounded metal tip, meant for a bow. When Jim first gave him this, David was only eight or nine years old and practiced in the walnut orchard where Jim lived in Lakeport. Jim saw his kids every weekend then. He probably shouldn't have moved back to Alaska. But what he remembers most is that David shot his arrows straight into the sky to see how close they would land. Jim never stopped it, because he thought it was funny. Real risk, possible death seemed so much further away then.

David raises the crossbow to his shoulder, takes aim at their fence, and fires. It's too fast to see. The arrow stuck in the fence, hard sound of wood, and a memory of flight.

"Holy shit," Gary says and laughs.

"I didn't realize," Elizabeth says. "That's not good. I thought it was just a toy, something that would kind of lob it in the air a bit."

David is looking at Jim, proud, waiting for his father's approval. Is everything we want and need this clear, in every moment, if only we could see?

"Hey hey," Jim says. "That was something. You would have been useful back in medieval times."

"Sir Darvid of Van Amberg," David says, and sweeps his arm as he bows. So strangely similar to Jim's own grand gesture of exit earlier today. Are we all controlled from somewhere else, puppets without visible strings? How could these two gestures happen, and only today, never before? He has no memory of either of them doing this in the past.

"My brother," Tracy says. Pride at eight years old, and what is that? What the fuck are any of them doing here?

"Well," Jim says, and then he doesn't know what should follow. What's the plan?

"Wanna try?" his son asks, and this seems perfect, a distraction, something to do.

"You bet," Jim says, and he takes the crossbow, which is fairly heavy, pushes up the nail trigger and pulls the bands, which are like Jim himself, stretched and held back. The feeling of all that potential energy. When he holds the crossbow, he can feel it, physically, the tension. A lightness to the power. He wonders about the physics of it. Does something under tension actually lose weight?

David hands him the arrow and Jim fits it in the slot. Gary should stand against the fence, and Elizabeth in front of him, in close, then David in front of her, and Tracy. Jim will set the crossbow in place, tie a string to that nail and go join them, in front, to feel the first piercing. They can all be linked, held together as one body, a family. In order to include Tracy, the arrow will have to come in low, at his belly.

Jim lifts the crossbow to his shoulder. He likes this too much, the feeling of power. When nothing can be controlled inside, that's when a trigger is most beautiful, most perfect. The .44 magnum takes only the lightest touch to release all that powder behind a heavy slug, a kick that feels like it could break your wrists. The slug will stop a grizzly at close range, knock it back and tear a hole in its chest.

The crossbow has no sight, the leather pouch resting too high, making it impossible to see the arrow. And a nail is not as satisfying as a trigger. Jim realizes that if one of these bands ever fails, it's going to snap back into the shooter's face and probably blind him, but he knows that won't happen right now, because he's cursed with an empty world without event.

Nothing will take over and determine what he should do or who he should be. All the world is only waiting.

He aims at the fence because where else would he aim, and he pulls that nail down and the arrow is there in the fence again. Such a strange release, the opposite of a gun. No kickback but instead the bow pulled forward. No punishment but a load taken away.

"Can I try?" Gary asks. "That thing's a trip."

"Do you like it?" David asks.

Jim wants to respond, but he feels lost. He hands the bow to Gary, and nods to David, hoping that will be enough. If he speaks, he's afraid his face will break and show too much. So he stands and watches his brother shoot, and he wants a time mover, something to make it all pass smoothly, something to keep him out of it. He shouldn't be responsible for its workings.

"You haven't seen my present," Tracy says.

He's happy to have a reason to move.

"I can see now," he's able to say.

She grabs his hand and tugs, pulling him through the garage into the house, to the living room with its brick fireplace and low ceiling, a sliding glass door looking out to pine trees.

"Close your eyes," she says when he's sitting on the couch, and he closes them gladly. You don't have to respond if your eyes are closed. Everyone will let you have a blank face, a nothing face. It's the only time we can be free around others. A gulf banded with leftover light and he's sliding to the side, falling in waves of pressure, his pulse. The heart could be only a foot away or this could be on the scale of planets, rings of

Saturn and such. Impossible to measure distance inside, no reference, only our sense of things, insanely variable.

"You can open now," she says, and when he does, he sees a drawing of the two of them, walking slanted in a world where there is no ground. His body without flesh, made only of sticks, and his face simple, a circle, happy to match hers. Their stick hands joined in a jumble of crayon, and this must be what we feel when we touch someone we love. It would look like that if it were visible.

"I love it," he says, and he does. He's always lied about his children's art, but this time he does love it, a gift of the depression, that there are moments of clarity, of purity, and he can respond more directly to the world than he ever has before. "I love that there's no ground," he says. "Just the two of us, holding hands. Not coming from anywhere and not going anywhere. There's only the sun and the feeling we have when we hold hands."

"I love you, Daddy," she says and wraps her arms around his neck. The innocence of it makes him feel so sad. He closes his eyes and clings to her.

"Jim," Elizabeth says.

"You're crying, Dad," David says. "Why are you crying?"

"Sorry," Jim says, and he lets go of Tracy, stands up, wipes his eyes. "I just haven't been sleeping enough. Just tired."

What's true is that he has no control now. Different feelings are getting him all day and night, and never any warning, no idea what will be next. It's terrifying to have no control, especially in front of his children. He doesn't like at all that they're seeing this.

Elizabeth is beside him, holding his arm. "Would you like to lie down and rest?"

"No. No. I'm fine. Let's go hunt for quail. Red-eye?" He tries to say this last bit to David with more energy. David nods but still looks worried.

Jim starts walking toward the front door. If he can make it outside, that will be better, the ceiling too low in here and also the air too warm and closed.

"You forgot your present," Tracy says, so he turns and she hands him the drawing and he takes it in both hands to keep it safe, makes it down the hall and out the front door. The sky still heavy. He wants to rise up into it, wants to not be held to the earth.

They drive into low hills, fancy houses set far apart. A few private vineyards, rows of stumps just starting their spring growth. Spring is so much further away in Alaska.

It's a paradise, this place. He can see that now. Oak trees and shade, narrow winding lanes, all newly paved by the rich, and so much open space. Not wild, not a place to hunt, but he asks Gary to pull over when there's no house in sight, and they all get out.

A wooden fence meant only for looks, just one heavy log low and one high, very easy to duck between. A fallen oak wet and covered in white lichen, or is it something else? Does lichen grow only on rocks? So delicate, like lace all along the dead bark. But is all bark dead, even on a living tree? What is it that's alive about a tree? How is it he knows so little at almost forty? His birthday is in three months, if he makes it that long, but he knows he won't. He'll die at thirty-nine, a more awkward number. They'll say he was forty, just to keep it simple, or "almost forty." Gary will speak at the funeral. He's the executor of the will, so he'll be doing everything, including fighting the IRS to keep the few assets away from them. That won't be easy. Jim is leaving his brother with a terrible job.

David has been talking this whole time, but Jim hasn't heard a word. He knows only that there's talking and that it doesn't matter. And he should care more but he can't. He's watching the dark red meat of the tree where termites have opened it up. So much like flesh. Why do trees have to have skin too, with their sap and raw meat hidden beneath? Why did there have to be that correspondence? Why doesn't the sky also have a skin? Earth does, and just as changeable as human skin, always shifting, but more slowly. He'd like to understand something before he goes, something about all of it.

Gary has a hand on his shoulder now, so he must stop ignoring everyone. "Okay there, buddy?" Gary asks.

"Yeah," Jim says. "Just looking at how beautiful this is and wondering why it has to have skin like us. And why doesn't the sky have skin?"

David is looking at him intently. Standing there in his rain gear like a little man, holding his pellet gun. "The sky does have a skin, if you look at it upside down," David says. "The atmosphere is the skin, in a few different layers, and then outer space is the meat. We've been studying it in science. There's the troposphere, which is what we live in, then the stratosphere after seven and a half miles, then the mesosphere and thermosphere. Heat is the last thing, and space isn't far away. Less than two hundred miles. If we could drive on a highway straight up, we'd be there in three hours."

"Wow," Jim says. "I like that idea, driving into the sky. It would have to be a convertible. A fifty-five Olds, red and white. Remember those?"

"That's before my time," Gary says.

"Well they were the thing. I'd have my arm resting on the door, driving with one hand, heading for the stars. The sky would get darker, an intense blue like winter in Fairbanks, the sky the richest blue you can imagine, cobalt or navy or royal or something, I'm not sure what they would call it."

"It would have to be night," David says. "Because otherwise it would just get brighter and you'd get cancer from the radiation. And even at night, if you went far enough you'd leave the shadow."

"Like father like son," Gary says. "How old are you? Thirteen? I've never had any thoughts like that, even now."

What Jim realizes then is that his son could end up with the same depression and mood swings and endless unstoppable thoughts about his life, second-guessing everything. Mental illness a curse to pass down through generations. When did it begin in the past, how far back? And how many new generations will suffer?

Tracy laughs, that kind of low nothing laugh kids do just to be delightful and get attention. She has no idea what's going on, but she wants to be a part of it. So he reaches down and takes her hand. "Do you want to drive up into the sky, Tracy? Take a nice car and just drive straight up?"

She looks worried, and he can't tell if it's because she doesn't understand or because she does understand and believes it might be possible and they might do it, which would of course be terrifying. "It's only a joke, sweetie. No one can drive into the sky. So we won't be doing that. We're just going to walk here and look for quail."

"Did you believe it?" David asks her.

"Be nice to your sister," Jim says, but David is laughing.

"You believed people can drive into the sky!"

"Shut up," she says, and Jim doesn't have the energy for this, so he walks forward over ground that has been grazed.

46

Cow pies black and rippled, grass chewed, ground rutted by hooves during rains, every opportunity for weeds, thistle spreading wide spiny leaves to steal the sun. Laced with white, an indication of poison. It doesn't have any that he's aware of, but it's following the pattern of brightly jeweled spiders and snakes and frogs that announce their poison, and the showiness must be enough, along with a few spines. No thistle has been touched. All free to grow.

Are there any signs in Jim? If he walks past someone on the sidewalk, someone he's never met, can they tell he's poison? That's a problem with humans. There's no sign at all. No warning. It's a time his family should help him, but the safest for all would be if they stayed away. The solution would be to strip him bare of possessions and set him walking in an earlier time, before fences or roads, let him walk from here to the other coast, three thousand miles, and by then the poison might be out of him. He needs something as extreme as that, something as elemental and basic and external. He can be fixed only from outside, by doing. Thoughts have failed.

He's beneath another oak, black oak, dark pitted bark in patterns ancient and unreadable, grown twisted out of the ground. Heavy arms flung wide, like a man staggering and bent, but no weight visible above, only the sky. Torment without source but shaping nonetheless.

A scrub jay high up, roughest call of the blue jays and largest body, banded in black. Jim points at the bird. "Shoot that one," he says, because he knows David must be near.

He hears the pumping of the air rifle, seven times, max pressure, and the tiny bolt slid back, a pellet inserted. A pause as his son aims, then the spit of air and sound of impact, feathers loosened in the scrub jay's chest. The delicate inner lace, a whiter blue.

The bird goes straight down. No flapping or struggle, a shot straight to the heart. "Good aim," Jim says.

David is rushing to where the bird lies on its back. Jim takes his time, feels that he's a giant, that his steps are slow and can sink into the earth.

Tracy is there too, squatting beside the bird, using a thin stick to poke at it. She's wearing a pink shawl, something knit with big spaces. He didn't notice it before. He thought she was wearing rain gear.

The bird has shat itself, a light brown ooze that looks squeezed from a tube. Legs thin and dark. Beak and eye closed. Tracy is poking at the breast, mini CPR but lazy, without any real interest in saving. Can children believe in death, even if they see it?

"We should fry up the breast," Jim says. "I've never tried scrub jay. I don't know why I've never tried it."

"You can't eat scrub jay," David says, looking up at his father.

"Yeah," Gary says. "Just leave it there."

"No," Jim says. "We're going to try it. This bird gave his life for us. We shall partake of his noble breast."

David laughs. Jim looks up into the sky, closes his eyes, and raises his arms. "Scrub jay maker, thank you for this gift."

David and Tracy are both laughing now. Gary is not. "Enough of that," Gary says. "Let's move on and look for quail."

Jim kneels beside his children and takes the scrub jay in his hands. He plucks the feathers from the breast, quickly, smelling the stink of the bird, the oil in the feathers.

"I can do it, Dad," David says, and so Jim hands it over. His son finishes plucking, then rips the hinge of the breast open, scoops out the guts. Smallest heart and liver and entrails, fit for a doll's house.

"We don't need the whole thing," Jim says. "Just the breast. Slice off one piece on each side." He hands his pocketknife to his son, but David is already pulling out his own, red Swiss Army. Cutting small filets with bloody fingers.

"I'm thinking a red wine reduction," Jim says. "What do you think, Gary?"

"Yeah," Gary says. "Finish with some truffle oil."

"White truffle oil."

"Yeah." Gary has his hands in his pockets, looking down at the ground and kicking at a thistle, ignoring the warning signs.

David holds the two filets in his palm, dark meat. What our own flesh might look like if we cut away small chunks.

Jim stands and feels dizzy. The sky and clouds tilting out of unison with the earth. Edges revealed, misaligned, like a montage in an old movie. "Quail," he says. "We should hunt for quail. That's what we're doing here."

And so they walk on, fanned out over the land, waiting for the thrum of wings to erupt at their feet, listening for the sucking sound of quail hiding, looking for small bluish bodies and dark topknots.

"We should go uphill, where there are more trees," David says, and so they do that, following the curve of the land skyward. Jim could survive if all he had to do was walk, away from cities and other people, just walking from one tree to the next.

So much thistle and doveweed. All good grasses gone. Wide leaves of spine or velvet spreading over the broken earth, and the stink of them, all so we can have more hamburger. Clumps of poison oak, also uneaten.

The wind picks up and they feel the first drops. "You need to wear your rain gear, Tracy," Jim says. "Where's your rain gear?"

"It's in your hand," Gary says, and Jim looks down and there it is, a small blue rain jacket.

"Okay," he says. He kneels down and helps Tracy put in one arm and then the next, still wearing the odd pink shawl underneath.

"I can do it myself," she's saying, and he realizes how big she is. It was crazy that he picked her up earlier. She's not a young kid anymore. How did she become eight? And yet she's still making him drawings. He doesn't know where to place her.

"Sorry," he says.

"It's okay, Daddy." This bright look on her face suddenly, a feeling he can't imagine having. Her eyes so blue and large and flawless.

He can't look anymore, so he keeps walking, head down against the rain, sound of it falling all around. Much louder than he remembers. Loudest on leaves, a smack, but he can hear it hitting earth too, brutal. His boots slipping a bit in mud and slick cow pies. He steps in anything, curious how it will feel. The ground so dark and the sky gone, only cloud in close, a dirty white, and why not pure? How do clouds become gray?

"Hey," he hears. Some other voice, from behind. He turns, sees a man walking toward them. Wearing a brown jacket, old-fashioned oilskin. Yellow Carhartt pants. He raises one arm.

"Now we're in the shit," Gary says quietly.

"What will happen?" David asks in a whisper that is too loud.

"Nothing," Jim says. "Nothing ever happens." He steps toward the man, to bring fate closer, to speed things up. The man should be carrying a shotgun or rifle, out to protect his land, but he has nothing. Jim also has nothing. He's left the .44 magnum in Gary's truck. So they will have to use their fists or sticks and stones, beating each other to bloody pulps until one gives out. This is what Jim wants, some contest, no more dodging ghosts in his head.

The man is too old. At least twenty years older than Jim, and moving slowly. He seems to regret his task, doesn't have enough will to fight. This is a disappointment.

"Yeah?" Jim asks when they're within easier earshot, twenty paces apart.

The man stops, looks baffled. He spreads out his arms, hands open. "Well you're on my land."

"Yeah," Jim says.

"We were just hunting for quail," David says. "But we didn't find any."

"That's enough," Gary says to David. "Let your dad handle this."

"Handle what?" the man asks. "You're on my land, hunting illegally. You need to leave. I could call the police."

"We took one scrub jay," Jim says. "We carved its breast, in two pieces. You can have one. We can share our kill. Show him the pieces, David."

"What?" the man says. "I don't want a piece of scrub jay. Are you crazy or something? Just get off my land."

"Are you carrying a firearm, sir?" Jim asks.

"What the fuck," Gary says. "Why are you asking that?"

"No, I'm not," the man says.

"Well maybe you should next time," Jim says.

"Don't tell me what to do. Just get the fuck off my land."

Jim looks at the man, his weak mouth and worried eyes. He feels like he has all the time in the world. There's a kind of opportunity here, if he could just understand what it is. So he steps closer. His boots paw at the earth, and the man steps backward, puts his hands out as if he's ready to catch a basketball, so strange.

"Stop, Jim," Gary says, but Jim does not stop. He will walk until some external force finally intervenes. He will walk through man and walls and trees and fences, anything that gets in his way.

The man turns and runs, a weak hobble, his feet slipping in the rain and new mud, and Jim knows he could be faster, could run him down, tackle him and beat him to death, but he likes the feel of walking, wants only to walk, nothing more.

Gary grabs his arm, holds him back, so much stronger. "We need to get out of here now," Gary says in a low voice. "The cops will be coming. And you're doing this in front of your children."

Jim still is trying to walk, but he's held back. He likes the feeling of that, likes being determined from outside, wants the gods to reach down with thin fingers of steel and keep him in place.

"Your children," Gary repeats. "What are they supposed to think of this?"

Jim tries to care. He tries to feel something, tries to reach to wherever feelings are stored. That must be somewhere inside him. But he can't find anything, or even why anything is wrong. Why is it wrong for them to see this?

"It's like there are no rules now," he tells Gary. "Or reason or what I'm supposed to do. If I tackle that man and beat him on his own land and kill him, that's the same as never touching him. It's no different. And it doesn't matter at all that it's his land. It isn't his land. The idea is ridiculous. And the police are ridiculous. What are they doing? How do they know what to do and what not to do, and why should I care about them?"

"You'll care about them when they beat you with a night stick."

"Or maybe not. Maybe I'd like it. I don't know."

"You wouldn't like it."

Jim wonders how it would feel, to be beaten like a dog, and then he's down on all fours in the rain and mud, and he takes off at a four-legged gallop for the man, who is still not too far away, still slipping and righting himself like a ship at sea. Jim's hands stinging from thistle and rocks and whatever else, but he loves the feel of this, running with his shoulders, the easy lope of it, natural, his head hanging and mouth open, breathing hard, slavering. Only his knees too weak.

He tries to run on his feet and hands, keeping his knees from touching, but he falls forward, rolling, then uses his knees again.

He can hear David laughing, yelling that he's doing it too, but Jim doesn't look back. He's immersing, finally, into something better, into movement and breath and mud, exactly what he needs. No therapist in an office, just this. Running down the man in the brown jacket. He'll bite a leg first, fell him, and then he'll go after the neck. He wants the man's neck in his teeth, wants to clamp down and taste blood. And he's gaining. He's faster on all fours than he ever could have imagined, and stable, but the man is terrified. He falls, takes too long getting up, and the gap is closing. The thrill of this. Jim can feel his chest, how powerful he is, the muscles working.

But then he's tackled, swept from the side, held face upward to the sky, his arms and legs dangling useless, and he tries to punch at his brother but Gary's arms are in the way, tries to kick but now his legs are trapped. So much stronger. All he can do is stare into the sky as the rain comes down, open his mouth, and let out some low moan he doesn't recognize. What it means, who can tell?

Gary pulls him back to the truck and they take off fast. Jim wet in his rain gear, head slumped down into the green rubber, fisherman's slicker, smell of it and he could be at sea again. Coves in southeast Alaska shrouded always in fog, the water gray, but looking down he might see a hundred salmon, dark bodies aligned and perfectly spaced and without thought. Water so cold and clear. Shadow forms of ridges below them, outcrops, sand and mud and seaweed all indicated differently by shadings at depth, distorted by temperature bands.

This is what he's always loved, moments of purity, finding remote coves by boat, no one else around, or hiking far along a river with no trail to find a deep pool where steelhead have never been fished. The silence of those places. He wants to retreat now, doesn't want his children here, or Gary, or to hear the noises of a truck revving and thick tires carving turns. He doesn't want to think about what he's done or who he is or what any of it means. He wants to be without responsibility, without attachment, without consequence, without feeling except the basic awareness of sight and sound and smell in a place untouched.

But they won't let him hide. Grumblings from Gary, questions from David, and the most basic is the most difficult to answer: "What were you doing, Dad?"

The need to account for our lives, for everything we've done. What if we didn't need to? What if everything we've done is simply that?

"Song, sung blue, everybody knows one," Jim sings. "Song, sung blue, da da da da da da. Me and you, a number two, with a cry in our voice, ba dum dum dum dum, is that right?" He can't remember the words. "Help me, brother."

But Gary is gripping the wheel in both hands, driving very fast along curves and dips and rises, trying to get to a main road, probably. Hard to be faster than a phone.

"We've really got no choice," Jim continues singing. "We've got no choice." But he doesn't know if these are the words. Maybe they're only his words.

"I was crawling too," David says. "But you were going really fast, like a werewolf."

"I have to pee," Tracy is saying, and maybe she's been saying this for a while, because her voice is at high distress now.

"We should pull over for Tracy," Jim says. "She has a bladder the size of a peanut. I know from when I moved from Anchorage to Fairbanks. I had to stop maybe fifty times for her each way, and we did a few trips. What a pain in the ass."

Gary is saying nothing, though, only driving way too fast, concentrated.

"You were just like a werewolf, Dad."

"Ahoooo," Jim howls with his head back, and it feels right with the tires slipping and getting air on the rises. He's never seen his brother drive like this.

"Personally, I don't care at all if we're caught," Jim says. "Because what's going to happen, little brother? We walked on some guy's land, and then I crawled in the mud. Wow. What a terrible crime. And if they get really detailed in the investigation, we carved the breast of a scrub jay. I'm sure that comes with a life sentence."

Gary slows a bit. "Maybe you're right. I'm driving too fast. This is dangerous."

"Yeah."

"Okay. I'll slow down. Normal speed."

The tires become heavy again, attached to the road, and the turns are without so much g-force, whatever g-force is.

"What's g-force?" Jim asks. "Does it just mean gravity?"

"Yeah," David says. "Two g's means twice the force of gravity."

"Voilà. It's been worth it sending you to school. Better than having you work the crops and milk the cows. We had to sacrifice a bit, no Christmas oranges for three years running, and your ma had to make jeans out of wood, but we got by and it shore is worth it."

David is laughing. Gary is not.

"What's wrong, little brother? Cat steal your milk? Not seen your Christmas orange in nary a long while?"

"Manic," Gary says. "This is the manic part. You're on a high now, and it's way too high, as in crazy."

"I took a pill already though," Jim says. "So I'm saved, right?"

"The pills take a couple weeks, and he warned us they might just make everything worse during these first two weeks."

"Well that doesn't sound safe."

"No, it doesn't."

"I have to pee!" A wail of despair now from Tracy, who probably is barely holding it in, so Gary pulls over and she hurries out, hopping, gets her pants down, hiding behind the door, and they all hear her water on the roadside gravel, a bonding moment for a family.

"All distress gone," Jim says. "Taken care of so easily. We just have to find a way to piss out who I am, leaving a happier something else."

It seems to be more and more true that his utterances are met with silence. Perhaps that's the clearest sign of crazy. But it doesn't matter, which is the other sign of crazy. He feels he should make an effort, though.

"Seriously," he says. "The warnings Dr. Brown gave, they were missing something."

"What?" Gary asks.

But then Jim realizes he can't say this in front of his children, can't talk about the risk of killing others before killing himself. We're supposed to protect children, right up until whatever terrible moment in which we no longer protect them. Like telling David about the divorce. He was five or six then and still probably knew it was coming, without really knowing. Just announced one morning, sitting in the living room, the view out to Clear Lake, a nice rental on the water they had that year, after leaving Alaska. So much warmer in California, and the lake was glass. Jim was thinking of waterskiing while Elizabeth said the words.

So is this what we all want, to not be told until it's too late? If he decides to kill Rhoda, should he tell her ahead of time or would she not want to know until the last possible moment, the gun raised and just one word, yep, to confirm it, then pull the trigger?

He wants it to be like in the Dirty Harry movies. In the hotel room, she should be wearing lingerie and standing by the bed or even on it. She should take off her bra and her tits hanging there and he shoots one of them, the one over her heart, and a hole just appears, neat. Better if it's in a pool, more exactly like the movie, but that won't be possible, because if you kill one, why do you not kill others? Aren't his parents responsible also? Don't they deserve a visit? And what about his brother? A lot of open questions.

"Not much time," Jim says. "So much to think about. The big questions. And I mean the really big ones."

"Are we going to eat the scrub jay?" David asks.

Gary puts his hand on Jim's shoulder. "Slow down, Bud. That's all you have to do. You don't have to think about anything. Just let it all go. Nothing to worry about."

"Are we?" David asks again.

"Yeah," Jim says. "We're going to fry it up. We're going to Mary's now, right?"

"Yep."

"So yeah, we'll have dinner, and in one little skillet I shall personally prepare the noble breast."

David is laughing, but now Jim is thinking of porn and noble breasts. He's getting a boner and wants to jack off. He wants to be left alone. He wants to fuck Rhoda, but that's not happening this evening, so he needs a magazine at least. He has a couple in his duffel. He keeps his chin down inside his rain gear and can avoid conversation that way.

What is a body? Slick with sweat and rain, feeling hot and chilled at the same time, an ache in his groin. He puts his hands together in his lap, as if he's curled in close for warmth, but he's pressing against the boner. No one will know. Sex always secretive.

His shoulders feel strong, pumped from crawling, but the joint in his left elbow feels out of whack. And his knees are sore, crushed, and the pain in his forehead pulsing and soreness all around his eye caves, a tiredness there from months and months of not sleeping well, a deep fatigue. But Gary is right about the high, the euphoria. He's still riding it, a feeling that he could do anything, even step outside the truck at speed and fling it into the air. He can feel it in his veins, a chemical rush making him stronger, and this is nothing compared to what it does to the part of him that is not his body.

He wouldn't call it a soul, because that's a tired thing shuffling around in chains and having to sing hymns and attend potluck dinners. The closest he can come to naming it is to remember those moments fishing in Alaska. When he was alone on his boat in a cove and the world stood still. He could hear individual drips from the trees and the cool air offered no resistance. Some part of him was able to travel then, to fill larger spaces. He feels the power of that now, some force in him that can grow without limit.

The problem is that there's no goal, nothing to attempt. There's only sex, because there's nothing else. Sex is what's left, always. It will never end, and so perhaps it should be called the soul. Jim rubs at his boner in a way he hopes no one will see, and the hot ache of it makes him want to do terrible things, right now. He wants to stuff this into her mouth and cunt and make her swallow, and he wants to punish and master and make it known that he did not choose any of this. It was chosen for him and he objects.

"In the name of the father, the son, and the holy sex," he says.

"What the hell?" Gary asks.

"Just thinking of what is truly eternal, and that is our copulatory urge. That is what remains beyond us, our finest and highest calling."

"Think of your audience here."

"But I am. David should know. He should know as early as possible. He's already a man."

"This is only the euphoria."

"Euphoria is clarity, truth. Naming what can never be destroyed. Finding what it is in us that lives."

"Are you talking about sex?" David asks.

"Yes," Jim says. "Talking about the sacred. You won't find it in church. Everything there is dead and has been a thousand years. But you get a girl to come to your room when your mom's not home, and when you first feel her with your finger, how wet and soft and silky she is, that's when you come closest to what has made us."

"Stop, Jim. Tracy is hearing this too."

"I'm talking about source and origin. Reaching inside is reaching back. And the fact that you can be with girls only thirteen, or even twelve, just beginning, that's the most incredible thing. You'll never have that freedom again the rest of your life. So forget about everything else. I spent so much time on my homework and working at Safeway and going to church, being a good boy, but I should have been doing what your uncle did, just hanging out down at the pier at night with friends and beer and girls and putting all my life's effort into getting inside. It's the only goal, the only goal that matters."

"David," Gary says. "You have to understand your father is not well right now. He's not thinking straight. And Tracy, none of this is for you. Don't listen."

"Don't take away the only thing I have to offer. Right at the end, the truth. It's the gift of all the failure. I know now what doesn't matter, because I spent my whole life on it."

"Jim."

"Money, too, completely worthless. All I've made as a dentist. You need to know that, both of you, David and Tracy. Don't make yourselves slaves to money. And don't care what others think. Another worthless thing. Everything we're told, all our lives, ignore all of it. Listen only to me right now, your father trying to help you."

But of course they won't be able to hear, because that's the truth also, that we can offer nothing. No one can believe anything they haven't already learned. There's no transmission possible, no shortcut.

"We should take them back to their mother," Gary says. "Just have dinner ourselves tonight."

"No. I get my full time, crazy or not. Especially at the end. Don't take things away from me at the end."

"This isn't the end."

"I think you know."

Mary's house is small but tucked away in some trees off a less-traveled road. Mary thin and lovely, dark haired, Italian heritage, or Spanish. Suddenly Jim can't remember which, and he's too embarrassed to ask. But she's the kind of woman Gary has always gotten, more beautiful than the kind of woman Jim has ever gotten, not to compare or want to take a stone to your brother's head when he's out tilling his fields, but still, it creates this envy in Jim, the same as anger, not so far from rage, not far removed from the larger sense of unfairness and being fucked by everything in life and wanting to make some comment about that, some larger gesture and final, of course, and involving the magnum. Always back to the magnum.

He could shoot her right now, and then his brother, and then his children, then visit Elizabeth, then visit his parents. What holds him back? Not something that can be named. It doesn't seem to be anything at all, and in fact if he tries to feel it, it's not there. Nothing holding him back. He simply hasn't done it yet. It hasn't happened. That's all that can be said about why it hasn't happened.

"Hi there, Jim," Mary says. He's already standing in the driveway, not remembering when he left the truck or whether anything else has been said.

"I don't think I can say hi anymore," Jim says. "I've said it so many times in my life, and what does it mean?"

"Well just come in then, you silly goose," Mary says and takes his arm. Jim feels like he's eight years old. Mary teaches elementary school, and she's identified Jim's current emotional age right away.

A lot of rugs and throw pillows, stuff on the walls and counters, no free space anywhere. Jim feels claustrophobic. Owls made out of macaroni, crocheted kittens, children's drawings in crayon. Color everywhere, a storm of color like voices, manic, and he hasn't felt this before. It must be the medication, already fucking with him. Making everything worse for two weeks. How can that be a good plan? Brown said it can increase his symptoms and add new ones. And if he suddenly stops taking the pills, that's even more dangerous. Trapped on some narrow track going full speed toward something he knows can't be good.

Mary has sat him on the couch in the living room, and for some reason his children aren't here yet. Outside still with Gary.

"It would be so easy," Jim says. "Really, you have to know. I'm a danger now to myself and others. I could do it at any time."

Mary has a nervous laugh, smiles at him like he's made some joke, and then walks away to the kitchen. Can she really be that cowardly? How much warning does Jim have to give? Why is he not in a straitjacket?

"Did you hear me?" he says, and he realizes his voice is too loud.

"Oh Jim," she says in her voice for children.

So she really is completely incapable of dealing with him. And what about everyone else? How is his family supposed to help him? His children are too young. Elizabeth could maybe help, but she's no longer his family. Gary is trying but can't go where Jim needs to go. And his parents won't. Only Rhoda will go there, but everyone is trying to keep him away from her.

"What happens when it happens?" Jim asks. "What will you tell yourself then? Will you say, 'Oh Jim'?"

Mary's head shaking a bit, perhaps, as she looks down at the cheese and crackers she's preparing, but her concentration seems absolute. She is completely denying that he could have spoken or that she could have heard. Just the cheese and crackers. Arranging them in cute little rows.

"There," she says brightly. "You must be hungry." She sets the wooden cheese board on the coffee table, somehow finding space among all the colorful crap, the magazines and knitted things, things he can't even see he hates them so much, and then she walks away, without ever having looked at him.

His children and Gary still mysteriously absent, so he sits alone, has a cracker, whole wheat, a slice of cheese. Swiss, with holes, made with a shotgun. Do they shoot the cow while milking, to put the holes in the milk, or wait until later when they have the round of cheese? He imagines rolling them out of a barn, rounds of cheese as large as wheels, leaning them against hay bales and a line of men and boys with shotguns waiting for the command to fire. The way they shot pigeons in Tom Kalfsbeck's barn, one rousting inside and the rest waiting under the sky, four shots each, a shell ready in the chamber.

"The seas are so huge," David is saying as they enter, and Jim has a vision of the future, his brother becoming a replacement father for David and Tracy, taking them hunting and fishing and telling them nothing about a life or how it should be lived, same as other fathers.

"What are you talking about?" Jim asks, in a rare social moment, feeling some will suddenly to last a bit longer.

"The moon," David says. "We get to use the telescope tonight. You should see it. It's so cool."

"He's talking about seas on the moon," Gary says. "I used to know the names of some of them, names like Sea of Tranquility or something, but I can't remember now."

"They took a halibut up there once," Jim says. "NASA wanted to see how it would adapt. A big one, almost three hundred pounds, in its own special Plexiglas tank, and they set it on the ground to let it flop, to see how high it would fly."

"Jim," Gary says.

But David and Tracy are both listening as if Jim is delivering news of the Messiah. "Imagine its white underside against the white dust and ash and sand or whatever it is on the moon, looking identical, like a mirror image, and that dark topside looking like the moon from farther away, patterns like craters. Dark side of the moon, essentially. The halibut has been waiting for this meeting, waiting for millions of years, brought home, finally. Destiny. And then it hits both ends, hard, like wings, and the gravity is so much less. Even on Earth, they can launch a few feet above deck. But on the moon, this halibut flew."

"Wow," David says.

"That's right. The astronauts were supposed to measure how high, but their pole was only twenty feet. They saw it pass that two or three times, rising into thin air, wobbling like a great celestial jellyfish, white as milk, the underside that is so smooth and impossible, made of dreams."

"How long did it fly?"

"They don't know. None of them looked at their watches, and none of them could remember time or what it's supposed to be. That flight could have been minutes or hours. They can't say. And they can't remember when it first took off, the first few feet of it rising. For some reason, that's gone. All they remember is watching it fade into the sky above them."

"Whoa," David says.

"Silly goose," Mary says. "You can't bring a halibut to the moon."

"They did," Jim says.

"It couldn't survive up there."

"They didn't mean for it to survive. It was supposed to have one beautiful flight, is all. That's all any of us are meant to have. None of us survive. The most we can be is an experiment. Billions of us are for nothing, but then maybe one of us has some use. Just think of all the other halibut who lay flat on the bottom of the ocean all their lives and died there in a place far more frightening than the moon, hundreds of feet down under colossal pressure, the pressure of having a mountain stacked on top of you, and no light, and so cold, but this one halibut is brought up from that world, put carefully in a tank on a boat, brought to Ketchikan or Prince Rupert and trucked all the way to Florida, thousands of miles, or maybe they flew the tank. I don't know. They probably flew it in a cargo jet. And they take it to the launchpad and lift it up by crane, this tank held by straps being lifted alongside a rocket, hoisted up toward the nose cone. Just imagine that, clear Plexiglas with Alaskan water and this three-hundred-pound alien resting on the bottom, both eyes on one side of its head, looking more strange than anything we'll ever find in space. They lower that tank onto a kind of gangplank that enters the nose cone and wheel it in and strap it in place. And when the rocket engines ignite, the halibut is the only one who can take the pressure, all the g-force. Nothing at all compared to the pressure where it comes from. It's already flat and can't be flattened more. It was made for this trip. It doesn't mind the cold of outer space, and doesn't need to breathe. All it needs is Alaskan seawater and no heating, no special care. Just a bubble filter to oxygenate the water, and some food pellets. Best astronaut there ever was. And patient. No need for psychological tests or precautions or worries about whether it might go crazy or get listless and suicidal or miss family too much, no need for communication back home. The other halibut don't even know it's gone. No parades down there, no stupid ideas of heroes or sacrifice."

"Jim," Gary says. "Really, just sit down. The manic thing now, and you're scaring everyone."

"Just focus on the story. Think of that halibut cruising two hundred and thirty-nine thousand miles, and spaceflight is so easy for it. We don't know what we're made for. Who would have realized that a halibut is the best astronaut? You might not think at first about how well adapted it is to cold and pressure and darkness and endless time with nothing more than feeding off the bottom. You have to understand the beauty in finding what the halibut was meant for. When they finally arrive, the humans are essentially bonkers and on the edge of death, all fucked up from lack of gravity and normal human contact and sunshine and fresh air and from eating space goo and that orange drink, but the halibut is ready to go. But beyond that, not even worried about being ready or not, no thoughts at all, which is the best possible state of mind. No fear as some mechanical arm shifts its tank out onto the moon and then tips the tank. It sloshes out there, the first water to hit the moon, something that hunk of rock must feel, recognition of thirst or something like it, desire for things never known, just like when sexual desire first hits us, so foreign and strange and impossible, nothing like our previous experience, and even the air feels it, evaporation, a vacuum becoming air because of this water, feeling itself come into being, and to the halibut the place feels warm, easy, so light, a weightlessness it has never imagined, the most exquisite freedom. It flops not out of fear or any instinct it's known before but this time out of pure joy, as much as a fish can know that. It's not missing oxygen yet, has just been immersed, healthy and strong and now absolutely free. It hits both ends and knows flight, true flight, for the first time. Not restricted by the thickness of water. No resistance. Something no human has ever felt either, and no bird, to fly in an airless place, and without any suit. No barrier. Only the purest flight ever known, pure also because both its eyes are on the top side of its head. Any other fish would see the astronauts below, the lunar module, the surface of the moon, but not the halibut. It sees only emptiness above, undistracted, or maybe it sees Earth, a blue-and-white orb so far away, and knows the ocean is there, Alaskan waters, reaches for home, flops again against nothing to try to propel itself faster. What does a halibut think in that moment of flight? Until we know that, do we know anything?"

Gary is holding him, which is so strange, holding him from behind, hands on his biceps. "Let's just sit down," Gary says, and Jim does it. He feels exhausted suddenly, so exhausted. He lies back against the couch and closes his eyes, curls to the side.

"What's wrong, Dad?" David says, but this is so far away Jim can't respond. He needs to rest.

Tracy does her nervous cute laugh, and he'd like to reassure her, be a father, be normal and who he's supposed to be, but he just can't. How did he ever do it before?

They let him lie down in a bedroom until dinner. No attempt, strangely, to remove his muddy clothing and make him take a shower. Too afraid of him, perhaps.

His eyes the deepest sinkholes, caverns of ache, falling through to the backside of his head. Nose completely blocked, as usual, and throat raw from breathing through his mouth. He has trouble swallowing, and it's not possible to have the next breath until after swallowing. A kind of panic, trying to clear that tiny passage. His life passing through the smallest hole. All we are is breath, and he can never get one.

And thoughts, without end, his head never turning off. So tired they jump everywhere, his practice in Fairbanks at a standstill, patients all having their appointments postponed, over and over, death for a practice. He was going to bring on another dentist before he left, but the few he interviewed could tell. They knew he was not well.

And the ranch, whether the IRS will get it, whether he'll ever see it again, the feeling of hot air coming up the lower glades, blowing against his face and the hairs on his arms, pure pleasure, seeing the patterns in grass, swirls and eddies from several hundred yards approaching, closest sense of god visiting us. His father standing there fat and hidden away but perhaps feeling the same pleasure. Who can know? His father grew up on a farm in another time, only ten years after the first flight, long before TV and when the moon was only myth, not something that could be reached, and certainly not by a halibut. His father peeled potatoes, woke before daylight, ran traplines. What else?

Each of them a collection of myths but the gaps between the stories are enormous. Even what he knows of himself, even that is mostly gap, mostly unknown. Mary ignores every gap, forces a continuous story, one that all makes sense because it can't do otherwise, and to Gary it has never occurred that there is a story or not, and his children are the center still of every story and can't imagine any gaps yet, but they will when their father is gone. Jim's problem is that he can't enter his life, and he will pass along this problem.

What he needs is to jack off. The only time he can forget breathing and thinking. So he gets up, groaning, and reaches to the bottom of his duffel for one of his *Hustlers*.

The women are helping put out a fire, wearing large red firemen's helmets and little else, handling hoses in ways that don't seem focused on the task at hand. One is squatting down, her lips butterflied, and she looks so perfect, some airbrushed visitation from Mars or the pearly gates. A god he can believe in, Pussydon, god of the seas within us, endless water for any fire. Two of the women are having a water fight, nipples showing through wet, white T-shirts, hoses spurting into the air, and one of them is sitting on a thick dick, her leg held out to the side.

Jim's dick feels so satiny and soft, but the light touch is only at first. He squeezes then, really as hard as he can, and likes the ache of that, and then he's pumping beyond what's comfortable, because it's so difficult to come now. It used to be easy. He used to try not to come. But now he has to

yank as fast as he can, so fast his shoulder freezes up and the
end of his dick burns, and when he comes there's so little to
show, dried up from doing it too often. Purple and swollen
all around the head of his penis, bruised, painful, and the
skin below that torn a bit, just very small tears no more than
a couple millimeters, but they sting. Jim is out of breath,
gasping from the effort, not from pleasure. He feels so little
pleasure now, only need.

He wonders whether he was loud enough for anyone to
hear. He uses a tissue to clean the tiny bit of come, stuffs
his *Hustler* back down into the duffel bag, and tries again to
rest or even sleep. How amazing it would be to just sleep.
His heart hammering still, his arm and shoulder and dick
all pulsing, his head spiraling in pain. Smell of video porn
booths, that smell that comes from jacking off several times
without a shower between, something the semen does to rot
and transform. When do the good moments come, the ones
worth living for? When are they supposed to be? He needs
to talk with Rhoda, needs a plan for how to get through this
evening, because right now it feels impossible.

So he takes a shower. At least that's productive. Muddy
clothing crusted and flaking on the tile floor, and he steps
naked into water too hot and steaming, feels his skin burn,
watches it turn red, keeps having to step out of the stream
and then goes back, wants immolation but not dry. Hot water
one of the purest pleasures, but just a few degrees hotter and
everything changes.

He can't endure. He has to turn the temp down, and
it feels good to go all the way to cold, because his skin is
superheated now, residual cooking, but then he's coughing,

weak from no sleep, and he turns off the water, grabs a towel
that is too old and rough, has to pat himself dry carefully. It
hurts too much to rub.

He leans his head out the door and yells, "Hey can I bor-
row pants and a shirt?"

Why bother getting dressed at all? The daily actions, the
routines, he hates the whole circus. How many meals has he
eaten? A thousand every year, at least, so forty thousand times
chewing through what mostly was unwanted, only necessary,
peanut butter and jelly sandwiches, pasta, canned soup, some
dry piece of meat, and how many times taking a shit? Maybe
fifteen thousand times? A hundred thousand pisses? Taking
clothes on or off at least thirty thousand times.

And how many swallows, how many breaths? Mostly we
are machines, working pieces of meat.

A soft knock and Mary's voice, wavering: "I have a pair
of Gary's jeans here, Jim, and one of his shirts." So he opens
the door, standing there in his towel, and she doesn't look at
him, just holds her hand out, head turned away, and he takes
the clothing, closes the door again.

Soft old clothing, worn jeans and flannel shirt, too big for
him. Smell of detergent.

He walks out like a shrunken old man no longer fitting his
previous self. Something diminished and barefoot.

"We have to get you some socks," Mary says. "And slippers."

"I need to call Rhoda," Jim says. He's in the hallway at the
edge of the living room. Mary has disappeared for the socks,
but Gary and David and Tracy are all watching him.

"That's not a good idea," Gary finally says.

"I need a plan," Jim says. "How to get through the evening."

He doesn't like that David and Tracy are hearing this, but there's nothing else he can do.

"Everything's fine," Gary says. "We're just going to have some dinner here. And maybe we can play pinochle after."

"The plan's not like that."

"Well what kind of plan then?"

Jim feels the enormity, the impossibility. Why does he ever think there can be a plan?

"Can we play pinochle now?" David asks.

"Okay," Jim says. He will try not to scare his children.

The dinner table is already set, so they use a folding card table, brown, just like the one Jim has up in Fairbanks. Same brown folding chairs, plastic over metal. He will kill himself at his card table. If it happens when he's back up in Alaska, that's where he always sits. No other furniture. So he'll be in a chair just like this, at a table identical, the .44 magnum resting on it, loaded, and he'll be talking with Rhoda on the phone. He'll call her and she'll probably be at work, or with her new boyfriend, or otherwise busy, and she won't be able to hear him well. He'll say, "I love you but I won't live without you." Or maybe "can't" instead of "won't," because really is it any choice? And she won't hear and he'll have to repeat it, all things made small in the end, the utter lack of dignity on our way out, and then he'll pull the trigger and much of his head and blood will be instantly on the ceiling and walls but he won't have to see it, won't have to see or feel or know anything else ever again. All suffering gone in an instant, and so why has he delayed?

Gary deals him cards in threes, and this seems right. Nothing clear in life. You'd never be dealt a single card, always two other ways you might go. He arranges them by suit, has more diamonds than anything else, only one heart, his life with money and no love, and this is both a weak hand and a strong hand, no help to his partner but he might take the lead. Is anything neutral? Can cards just be cards? What will it be like on the other end of the phone? What will the gunshot sound like, and will there be dripping afterward, pieces of him raining from the ceiling? Will she ever answer a phone to that ear again? And will his death become more important than the death of her parents, or will that murder and suicide remain primary?

"Your bid," Gary says.

But Jim hasn't heard anything. "Where is it at?" he asks.

"Twenty-seven to you."

"Twenty-seven then."

David is his partner across the table, eager, watching him. He must have already bid once, which means he has at least a helping hand.

"It's to you," Gary says, but Jim has missed the bids again, has no idea what anyone has said. Mary standing there holding her cards in one hand, not sitting because she's still prepping the food.

"I'll bid," Jim says. "Whatever the next number is." Not one of them has ever done this in their entire family history of pinochle, but it seems to work fine, and Jim ends up with the bid. "Diamonds," he says, and he notices that Tracy is sitting close beside him, watching his hand. He puts an arm around her. "Do you think we'll make it?" he asks her.

She smiles and bounces on her seat in response, but no words, which is fine with Jim. He'd like everyone to stop using words.

David passes four cards. The missing ten is there for the run, and even the two aces he needed, but Jim does not feel excited. He lays down the run and aces to pleased bobbing and expression from everyone, which gives him a moment to hide. He can play pinochle without thinking, passing losers to David, picking up his cards again, and playing out the lead ace as he has always done in how many thousands of hands, then his singleton ace of hearts, then the queen of diamonds to flush the higher trump, all ordered, and why have they played this for so many years? Were they really not able to come up with anything else to fill the time? Is everyone in fact on the edge of suicide all their lives, having to get through the day with card games and TV and meals and so many routines, all meant to avoid any moment of coming face-to-face with a self that is not there?

Dinner another vacant exercise. Venison, from the most recent kill, five months ago in the fall. Jim was there. Gary firing on the run, in the trees just above the reservoir. Huge scars left from his boots, soft dark earth and pine needles, and that little .243 up to his shoulder, the stock taped together, puny but accurate. Gary hit the deer with three out of four shots, peppered him. The buck tumbling and exposing more dark earth in a long slide.

That day was overcast, cool, later in the season, late October. All of them wearing brown jackets, disappearing against earth and trees. Jim will miss hunting. From whatever void or whatever happens after, he'll miss that return each fall, and Gary will be thinking about him. No void can be empty enough to take away all that we longed for or loved.

"What do you think happens after?" Jim asks. Surprised to hear his voice out loud, and wondering about the suitability of this question in front of his children. Not the model father lately.

"What's that?" Gary asks. He's at the other end of the table, looking subdued, head low, wearing a clean flannel shirt with the sleeves rolled up his thick forearms, a lumberjack.

"The afterlife, or not. What do you think it is?"

"Well," Mary says. "God has prepared a place for us, and Jesus will welcome us."

"But what happens?" Jim asks. "Step by step."

"We don't have to worry," Mary says. "All is taken care of for us."

"Like a resort where someone grabs your bag right from the taxi."

Mary looks uncomfortable. "Something like that. Yes."

"Who grabs the bag, and how did they get stuck in that role? If there's all this great service, someone has to provide it. Do they draw from the elf heaven?"

"Oh Jim." Mary smiles as if he's just being silly.

But there's no point in talking about heaven anyway. Suicides don't go there. Jim considers pointing this out, but he decides to hold back, because of his children. He can be appropriate still. He hasn't completely lost it.

In the past, suicide was considered a crime. Maybe it still is. Very funny, really, since the criminal can never be prosecuted. But family used to be responsible, at least for debts in debtor prisons, and maybe also for suicide. His son would have to pay the IRS, or go to prison if he couldn't manage to earn 365K at thirteen years old, and maybe he'd be hanged for the crime of suicide, an eye for an eye. At the moment, all law seems entirely fucked. Could be just his state of mind, but he can't think of a single law he believes in. Most of them come from the church. And why the sudden interest in law?

"What's the drinking age in heaven?" Jim asks. "You've got Europeans there, who are used to sixteen, and Americans used to twenty-one, so how does that get sorted out? Heavenly elixir must be powerful stuff, so you couldn't let just anyone drink it."

"Let's enjoy the food," Gary says. "It's a nice casserole, Mary."

"Thank you," Mary says.

In fact the casserole is incredibly salty, a pan of chicken and cheese goop with tortilla chips thrown in.

"I wonder about the architecture too," Jim says. "Some people say there's heaven and hell, but others add a purgatory, and I've even heard of a kind of waiting room for heaven, which would make four places. It's a crowd-control problem, like parking at a Giants' game, and where are these places, and how do you get from one to another? And what can you call you? If there's no body, how do you know what's you and what's not?"

"We have our souls," Mary says. "Each one special and not the same as any other, and the soul can never die."

"And it's okay that we can't feel the soul now, and don't know what it is? That will all be cleared up immediately afterward?"

Mary smiles, condescending, really as if Jim is eight. "Your soul is your goodness. You can feel that. You just have to let yourself."

"But what about the souls that go to hell? Are they also made out of goodness? And I don't even believe. What happens then, when you don't believe but you've been given plenty of instruction and had every opportunity and therefore are supposed to believe? What happens if the nutcases are right and there is an afterlife? I'm fucked if that's the case. Sorry about the language."

"Don't call Mary a nutcase, please," Gary says.

"It's okay," Mary says. "All you have to do is accept Jesus's love, accept that he died for your sins, to save you. That's all you have to do. You don't have to think about anything else."

"Is he okay with suicide?"

"What?"

"What are Jesus's views on suicide? Does he still love us then and save us? And what if we take others with us? Aren't there some limitations to Jesus's love? Or does he consider his own death a kind of suicide? I guess that could make him sympathetic. He did have plenty of warning signs and willed it to happen anyway, so yeah, I guess Jesus was a suicide like those guys who walk up to cops pointing a gun, but with a grander plan for the purpose of that suicide."

"Wow," David says. "I didn't know Jesus committed suicide."

"He didn't," Gary says.

"He did, in a way," Jim says. "And he wanted an attention grabber. No pistol to the head or pills or car exhaust in the garage or yanking the wheel on Highway One. He went for a long, drawn-out torture, a slow suicide that would be remembered."

Mary stands up. "You have to leave," she says. "You have to leave right now." And then she walks quickly to the hallway, toward the bedrooms.

"It looked like she was crying," Jim says. "Like she had tears."

Gary is already up and following her. "Yeah," he says. "Nice one."

Jim looks at David and Tracy and shrugs. "Let this be a lesson, I guess. Remember how weak the religious are. They're denying so much about the world they can't handle any contact with it. And I'm not going to apologize. Fuck her and her faith."

Tracy's face is crumpling, so he leans to the side and puts his arm around her. "It's okay," he says. She starts to cry, and he tries to console her, but he feels tired. He doesn't have the energy for this. And what is the crying about, anyway? Kids are such a pain in the ass.

David is upset, too, even though he's older. He's staring at Tracy across the table and getting some sort of crying contagion from watching her face.

"If we could stuff a hundred people in here, everyone would be crying soon," Jim says. "Why can't we have our own emotions? Let Mary cry alone. There's no need to join her. She probably cries whenever a piece of macaroni falls off one of her crap decorations."

"Why are you being mean?" David asks, and then he's crying too.

"Fuck me," Jim says. "I'll just go wait outside. Try to eat a few more bites so you don't show up at home hungry. I don't want to get in trouble there too."

He rises and leaves them to it, and everything in the room seems brown. The dinner table, the card table, the casserole, the doilies, the rug, various pieces of wood. All the wild color gone somehow, only brown left.

Outside, he's happy that the air is cool and the sky clear. He can see stars and the moon so bright. Even without a spotting scope, you can see there are huge craters and seas. He'd like to visit, but that seems unlikely. So limited what we get to experience. NASA should sign up suicides as volunteers. Jim would gladly get in a capsule that's not coming back. He could reach as far as Jupiter or even Pluto, be of some use to others and transcend a normal life. Why does that never happen? Why don't we send out capsules that won't return? Why are we so chickenshit and limited? What do we think we're preserving? Do we really believe one life is valuable? If we think about our experience for even one second, we know it's not. Heart attacks, car accidents, natural disasters, gun deaths, war: we're flicked away like ants in every moment. Clearly we have no value.

To pass through the rings of Saturn, to see them up close, that's what he wants, and to step on some other planet, with no spacesuit, just his jeans and a T-shirt. The video running and radio on so he can say what it's like, what it's really like, how the air feels, the temperature. He'll go barefoot and say what that feels like too. And it doesn't matter if he only lasts two or three minutes or even a few seconds in some burning place, because everyone else on Earth and all who are born after will know something more, everyone made richer through the sacrifice of nothing. Some will cry for him, some will have stupid ideas that he's a hero or an idiot, as if it matters what he is, and the religious will go off in twenty new directions of imbecility, new talk of how Jesus is fire resistant or doesn't need oxygen to breathe or Jim is the devil, vanished on Jupiter to reappear in all our bedroom closets that very night, but all will be made richer, and Jim will know more intimately what heaven and hell are like, because both must be airless places, and sound might not be the same, unable to travel, and though we believe hell is both on fire and freezing, who has ever said what the temperature of heaven is? Tropical for those who like the heat, but breezy and low seventies for those who prefer a mountain summer? Jim will be the first to report back, and others can follow. Some should go beyond radio range, starting out as children, because why not? Why shouldn't we see farther things?

What Jim would like is some use for his despair. Why can't his fucked-up state now be perfect for something?

But all he can think of is walking thousands of miles or traveling to space, one of them useless and the other impossible. He should pull a Mother Teresa, but the problem with the lives of the good is that everything moves so slowly, and he just can't bear it. Going out with a bang is much easier to imagine.

They're back in the truck again, one pointless trip after another, just a short way over the hill to Elizabeth's house, which Jim paid for, by the way. All the money he's spent in his life, all the waste, houses and building the commercial fishing boat that lasted only one season to be sold at a tremendous loss. Staggering to think of it all together. The problem was no reliable plan, just fits and starts all moving too quickly, the future always waiting with a surprise. You've bought a new red Mercedes convertible, but right before it's finally delivered by ship all the way to Ketchikan, your wife finds out about your affair with Gloria, so you drive it around Ketchikan's eight miles of road for one afternoon, then it goes back on the ship and you pay thousands in restocking, congrats. Or you buy a new Uniflite cabin cruiser, brand-new shiny gelcoat and upholstery and newboat smell and engine so perfect in its just-oiled haze and gleaming paint, then you forget to put in the drain plugs and it sinks the first day. You look at it submerged in maybe twenty feet of saltwater below the docks and you know everything about the boat will be fucked forever because of this. Mysterious electrical shorts hidden behind bulkheads, an engine that never hits full power because of residual rust in the cylinders, pumps turning on when no switch has been flicked, lights going out just as you need to come into the harbor at night, a VHF radio and other electronics that will need replacement on day two. You are master of your destiny. Kids you will have but not live with anymore and your son who will say no to a year in Alaska so you get to be the vacation father only, congrats. A second marriage you will fuck up the same way as the first marriage, by being unfaithful, because why not pay alimony to two ex-wives, and the kicker is that when you want to get back together with her she finds a poor fuck named Rich. And the tax dodges. That worked out magnificently. The IRS was fooled just long enough for all the penalties and interest to become something monstrous. And who knows what else. The expensive new house in Alaska, forgetting that, oh yeah, houses are supposed to have people in them, but this house is out of sight of any neighbor and you have no family up there and no wife or even girlfriend, and who are your friends? You have some down here in California, whom you aren't planning to visit this trip, oddly—Tom Kalfsbeck and John Lampson, why aren't you visiting them—but no friend in Fairbanks. Nice one on that. Good thing you made the house two stories with three bedrooms.

"I need to see John or Tom," Jim says. "What the fuck am I doing this trip?"

"Jim," Gary says. He's grim at the wheel, nothing new there, evergreens and various bushes swept by the headlights as he turns along this mountain road. Paved and faster, but not so different from the ranch at night.

"I'm going to see them."

"I'm not sure when we can fit that in."

"Tomorrow we go to Lakeport, and John is close enough. Then Tom on the way back down to Santa Rosa."

"It's not on the way to go through Williams and the Central Valley."

"Close enough. And when am I seeing Rhoda? When do we fit that in?"

No response, of course. And Jim should be paying more attention to his children. This may be his last time ever seeing them, this short ride over the hill and goodbyes that will no doubt be quick since everyone has been crying.

"Remember that money doesn't matter," Jim says. "David and Tracy. Remember that. Do something you like in life. Don't be like me. And try to be kind when you remember your dad. He didn't mean to be as fucked up as he was. You'll see when you get older. Sometimes a life just goes beyond your control."

Tracy is jammed in close next to him on the bench seat, and David between her and Gary, straddling the stick shift. Jim looks at both of them in shadows and light that keep sliding away, but they don't look at him. Both with their heads down, enduring, same instinct as adults when cutting someone out of the pack.

He has an arm over them, and he shakes David's shoulder until he looks. Jim grins. "Come on, son," he says. "Don't be hard on your dad."

David grins just a bit, still sad, and gives a nod, some acknowledgment but faint, just a tad more than you'd get from the wind or a pile of rocks. Jim curls his arm around Tracy and pulls her even closer. "I'll miss you, Tracy," he tells her, and then he's choking up, out of nowhere, eyes watering and mouth hung. "Even the monster feels something, eh?" he says, but he has trouble getting the words out.

Bundled so close beside his children who are so far away. And the time so short. They top the hill and descend into Hidden Valley, take just a few turns, up Rolling Hill Drive and down and there's the house. The life he's excluded from now. His own fault, but still exclusion.

"Don't forget me," he says. "Try to remember our best times, out hunting or fishing or skiing, wrestling on the carpet or playing pinochle. Think of times when I was happier, not the way I am now, okay?"

Gary has already pulled into the driveway and cut the engine. Elizabeth is out on the porch, and Jim has to open his door to let them escape. "A hug," he says. "Give your dad a hug." They pause long enough to do that, but not real hugs, not enough for the end, then they're gone and he's back in the truck weeping as Gary drives away. Such a weak sound, this choked little crying, so high-pitched. And the terrible feeling of loss, as if his children have been taken from him, as if they have died. A cavern inside him without limit. A stone would fall forever.

Gary's house is in Sebastopol, only twenty minutes away, on a steep hill dense with redwoods. A winding road without lights or traffic, then up the long private driveway, almost needing four-wheel drive. Log house at the top, built by Gary himself, blond pine. Big, two stories, peaked roof. The front part of the house on stilts because of the hill.

"We should sleep," Gary says. "It's been a hell of a day."

"Yeah, I'm exhausted," Jim says. "Not from the flights, but from everything here."

"Yeah," Gary says.

They walk in darkness to the house, Jim carrying his duffel bag and valise. Weight of the magnum still, always there. Shells in the duffel.

The air wet and cool. Stars visible, clouds mostly cleared away. The redwoods giant shadows above extending, leaving only small clearings of sky. Shadows so tall to remind us how far away everything is, unreachable. You'd think a tree above at night would be only black and flattened, but somehow it still retains its height even in darkness. We know the shape of everything beyond what we can see. The smell of redwoods, both sweet and acidic, and peaceful, memory of hikes and camping. He's often dreamed of living in a forest, but the truth is they're cold and damp. You never feel the sun. They're the worst possible places to live, except caves.

"You're lucky here," Jim says. "This place and house, and Mary."

"You could be too. You could live here with me for as long as you like, and you could find someone new, someone good who treats you well. And you could see your children every day if you wanted."

"I'll never see them again."

"Of course you will."

"No I won't. Or if I do, that will be bad. It's better if I don't see them again."

"What do you mean?"

"The warning Dr. Dickhead gave you was missing one important element, the what if our poor suicide becomes not so likable in the end and takes out others with him first."

"You'd never do that."

"I've thought about shooting Rhoda first. Imagined right where I'd shoot her, in the left tit when she's naked or wearing lingerie, standing by the bed."

"Jesus Christ, Jim, why the fuck can't you stop? Just stop thinking of this shit. Just remember we all love you and find small things that are pleasant. Go for a hike here in the morning, and we can play pinochle or watch TV. Anything to not go where your thoughts go. And I can't deal with it anymore tonight. I'm all done with crazy for today."

"Sorry. I'll try to stop."

"Thank you." Gary is opening the back door now, and they leave their muddy boots outside.

Gary doesn't say any more but just heads upstairs. Jim knows he won't see him again tonight.

So he has the whole downstairs to himself. Open front room with a twenty-five-foot ceiling, large stone fireplace reaching up to exposed timbers of the peaked roof. Such a grand feel, and amazing it's owned by a teacher. Soft thick carpet and a wall of glass to look out over the valley, acting only as a mirror now.

Jim lies down in the middle of the room, stares up at the ceiling so far away. He does snow angels. He wants everything to be soft like this carpet.

A mead hall. This could be a mead hall if it weren't for the carpet, if the floor were only wide planks of wood. And the insulation not as good, more wind coming through the walls. Jim could be a Viking, ready to die in battle. That would be no problem. Swing the ax and kill and hope to be killed.

There is an ax here, no doubt, and Jim rises to find it. He walks into the spare bedroom and checks the closet, finds clothing and a shotgun, a 12-gauge pump. Boxes of shells above, a few choices, from small birdshot to the big pellets for geese. Enough to take off a head without any problem at all. He loads three into the magazine and grabs three more to stuff into his pockets. Then he walks into the hallway, checks another closet.

Rain gear and boots, fishing rods broken down, small hand nets, and another shotgun, a semiauto. Jim has never liked these, because they jam. You try to take your second shot at a goose and there is no second shot. Pumps are more reliable.

But he takes the shotgun anyway, loads it also, wonders where the ax might be. Outside, in some shed? But he doesn't remember a shed.

Jim sets the shotguns on the dining table, barrels pointing at him. It would be a far reach to the trigger, but he could do it. The timing isn't right, though, something off. All the ache is there, missing his children, missing Rhoda, missing his life and any memory of what it was to be without pain, but this isn't enough. Some catalyst needed to make it all happen.

Gary appears above, on a kind of balcony upstairs to look down. "What are you doing with those shotguns, Jim?"

"Fair Rapunzel, let down your golden hair."

"What are you planning to do?"

"Nothing," Jim admits. "I guess I can't do it at your house. Something about what you would have to see, and the fact that this is your home. I don't know. I can hardly tell what holds me back or doesn't or pushes me forward. All hidden away, things not known until they happen. But nothing is happening here. I know that much. All just for show."

"Let's put the shotguns away then."

"No, I do like having them here."

Gary comes down the stairs. Jim has time. If he wanted to grab a trigger he could. But apparently he doesn't.

Gary takes both shotguns, holds them barrels down. "That thing Brown said about not letting you spend the night alone in your own room, I'm starting to see why he said that."

"But can you stay awake all night?"

"No."

"Then what good does it do? I need to be in a padded cell, with the door locked. That's the only real safety."

"Or you can just decide."

"Decide what?"

"Use some will. Decide to be strong. Decide to stay for your children and rebuild your life. Can you do that?"

"It's more like the weather. Can you decide the weather?"

"How about we start with tonight. I'm exhausted. I need to sleep. Can you just promise me we'll have breakfast together, that you'll keep yourself alive for that long?"

Jim considers this. Gary standing there holding the shotguns.

"Okay," Jim says. "If you take the pistol, too, and you sleep with all three guns in your bed so I can't get them. And your rifle too."

"I'm not going to sleep with all my guns."

"You are if you want me to promise. I mean the pistol under your pillow, so I'd wake you if I moved it, and the shotguns and rifle wrapped up in the sheets with you so I can't get them either. That's the only way I can promise. I know I'm not going to use a knife or look for pills. It will be a gun when I do it."

"The guns don't have some special power."

"But they do. And you know, from hunting. What they can do is irresistible. The trigger has to be pulled. Don't you want to pull the trigger?"

"No."

"Yes you do. You shot that last buck four times. Not just once."

"I was only trying to knock it down."

"Is that all?"

"Yeah."

"Have you ever picked up your rifle at night before sleep, held it to your shoulder and sighted in on some knot in the wall, or even your reflection in the glass?"

"I don't see what that has to do with anything, but yeah, plenty of times I've picked it up."

"And you still say it has no special power."

"That's right."

"What kind of dream is it, when you hold the rifle?"

"I'm awake. It's not a dream."

"A dream is happening then, all the stronger for being awake."

"Look, I'm going to sleep. I'll sleep with the guns. But no more mumbo jumbo. You're used to therapists now, but that's not how I talk."

"I'm talking about what you do, and what I do. Something real."

"Not real."

"So real I can't even say all the things it is. I'm several possible Jims when I hold a gun, and who knows which one will win. The feeling is so different for a shotgun or a rifle. Each with its own power, and every one of them makes me want to kill. Every one demands to be used. Every one offers an exit."

"You just said they were different."

"Yeah. They all kill, but the pistol wants my head. The .300 magnum wants my neighbor or someone in a car far away, or someone walking across a parking lot, and a pump shotgun wants a crowd in close. It was never about ducks or geese or deer. Just feel the weight of those two shotguns right now."

Gary closes his eyes. This surprises Jim.

"I do feel something," Gary says.

"Told you."

"But it's not like you say. I feel an obligation, to be careful, a responsibility."

"That's not the first thing you feel. Not the strongest, either."

"Yes it is."

"The fact that it wins doesn't mean it's strongest."

"Look, I don't even know what you're talking about."

"That's because you don't need the padded cell. But I do."

"Just give me your pistol now. No more of this shit."

Jim can feel himself smiling. "We come so close to the truth, little brother. I've had some amazing conversations with you today, you know that? We come so close to something, but then you always say it's nothing."

"The pistol."

"Fine." Jim grabs his valise, worn brown leather that's always made him feel he could be called Doc in a western. Pulling out teeth in a saloon, administering whiskey as painkiller. Everything real then. Bags made of leather, floors made of thick wood planks. He unzips the valise, hating that it has a zipper, something that wrecks the look, and he reaches inside and feels the instant something that can't really be described. The perfect smooth density of metal, its surprising weight, the compactness even of this enormous handgun with its long barrel, a kind of black sun with too much gravity. He holds it by the grip, finger on the trigger. "How can you deny what this feels like?"

"Give me the gun, Jim."

But Jim is grinning again, raises the barrel to the side of his head and pulls the trigger, hears the heavy roll and click.

Gary drops the shotguns and swings and this is the first time Jim has ever been punched in the face in his entire life, the popping sound of it, which could be his cheek or could be Gary's hand, and he's falling backward and feels some strange joy, a moment immersed. Fall that lasts so long and impact that takes all breath, and his head become a tunnel of sound. He closes his eyes and wants to enjoy this for as long as he can.

"You fucking stop right now!" Gary is roaring somewhere above him, calling on clouds to stop moving in the sky, asking the wind to settle, moon to hang still. The carpet so soft and the pain reassuring, clean, locatable and with a cause, a reason, and not something that will last forever.

"Thank you," Jim says. "This is nice. I feel a bit better."

His thigh kicked hard, a dull sensation that isn't really pain. "Damn you," Gary is saying.

"Yeah," Jim says. "I think that's already taken care of." But he doesn't want to talk, doesn't want to spoil the moment. He wants to enjoy. "Shh," he says. "I want to feel this." Eyes closed and the back of his head rolling softly on the carpet side to side, the comfort of repetitive motion, almost as good as being rocked to sleep.

His sinuses are jammed, though, and he can't breathe. It happens whenever he lies down, when he changes position. So he has to sit up, has to find Kleenex or toilet paper to blow, and Gary is gone already, the shotguns gone, his pistol. All reachable still, though, in that room upstairs, and his brother too tired to stay awake all night, and Jim will be awake, always awake.

He goes into the bathroom, grabs toilet paper and blows and gets some but not most. Ninety percent of it locked inside and pressurizing, like a car jack in his forehead being slowly cranked. He looks at himself in the mirror, a sick thing out of place among all the blond wood, the innocent walls. "Sorry," he says to the bathroom.

He should try to sleep now, so he goes into the chilly spare room lit by one bare bulb above, a mattress piled with old sleeping bags from hunting, no sheets or blankets. Thinner bags with red or blue plaid inside, and one of the enormous down bags from the army, dark green. He curls up in this, the reassuring weight of it and smell of steelhead and grouse, deer and geese and salmon and various boats, smell of bilge. He will try to rest, try to breathe and fall away.

Jim roams that night, unable to sleep, never able to sleep. Exhausted, feeling so heavy after several hours lying in bed, but some switch will never turn off. He's outside in the cold wet night air and still can't wake fully, lost in some half land, a taste of what purgatory will be, dark and cold and trackless and steep with the moon gone and shadows above. He descends, because this is easiest and where we're inevitably drawn, and he would like to lie down but he knows how many scorpions are here, hidden in all the deadfall. Purgatory vast, unlimited, no hordes of broken souls but each soul alone and afraid to rest because of all the small demons waiting. And what is the purpose, of purgatory or of this night? Is he supposed to be somehow made no longer himself?

All the surface loose. He can kick and send it spraying. Nothing solid. Sound of his descent, made small in the trees. The air colder and colder, coming closer to Satan and his maw frozen in the ice, so maybe purgatory is only where you think you've gone when you're descending to hell, the mind still playing tricks, still refusing.

No limit to the darkness inside us, no limit at all. Vast and unrecognized, unvisited. But he will visit now, or at least try. He holds his arms out and turns in place, slipping downward, and tries to ingest all of it.

"Satan," he says, calling to himself. "Come out come out wherever you are."

The air heavier, thick with chill, and everything wet, the trees and ground and air, all waiting to freeze, sinking toward where the beast is frozen to his belly. He was lunging from the water, exploding upward, so the ice is jagged all around him, spikes and arches and curved thin mountains that would be impossible anywhere else, all on a scale enormous. We could climb Satan and stand on an eyelash and still he would be too small for what waits inside.

Jim decides he will no longer follow the rules. He runs downhill but does not lean back to adjust for gravity. A kind of fall, weightless, and running his legs to keep up but he soars and doesn't know when the impact will come, all the world falling around Satan all the time, infinite collapse, and this is where Jim might meet himself face-to-face, fall into the mirror self, the one he can feel pulling at him day and night, keeping him from joy.

The hit softened too much by the leavings of the trees above, his face cushioned and body somersaulting, flipping into the darkness beyond but too brief and he's curled on his stomach and panting and wills the scorpions to come. A sting to wake.

But nothing happens, and this is always the problem. He will not recognize himself in this darkness, find his mirror self, the source of that tug, or the larger frozen form. Hell is unreachable. That is what is most cruel about it. If we could go there, we could finish and be reassured.

In the morning all his body aches from rolling sleepless in bed and perhaps also from the fall and being punched by Gary. Surprisingly his face doesn't look bad in the mirror. Perhaps he was made for a harder life.

His mind sore from wandering the same fruitless tracks over and over, thinking of Rhoda and all that happened. Tired thinking that goes nowhere. He will need to face his parents today, his mother's worry, judging him and saying "well" as she comes up against the wall of him. His father's silence in the other room.

Gary wakes early, so the two of them sit in the mead hall in dazzling morning light with a view over forested ridgelines all insanely clear after the rain.

"Ridiculous how beautiful that is," Jim says.

"You look tired."

"I'm always tired. I don't sleep."

"You should sleep."

"Yeah, I'll work on that. How was it sleeping with the guns?"

"Cozy."

They're eating cereal in large artsy bowls that must have come from Mary. Handmade ceramic with little nubbins that the spoon catches on. Pain in the ass. "Fuck these bowls," Jim says.

"You seem much better adjusted today. All fixed."

"Yeah. Mom and Dad will be pleased."

"They're afraid to see you. We're all afraid to see you. Nothing makes any sense. You have a good job and a lot of money, you're smart, you had a good wife and kids."

"Kind of a selective list, not really capturing all of a life."

"Only a few things are important."

"Nothing and everything."

"For one day try to be simple."

"The weather again. Snap my fingers and the sun blows out."

"Whatever."

"Yeah."

They go back to crunching. The redwoods shaggy and straight and with some agreement to share space, not extending their branches too far. A few birds visiting, long fall if they forget how to fly.

"Maybe I shouldn't see them," Jim says. "Save everyone the discomfort."

"You have to see Mom and Dad."

"But why? Why do we put up with obligation? Has anyone ever enjoyed it or received any benefit?"

"We're family."

"That's what I mean. Why torture ourselves?"

"Family isn't torture."

Jim laughs, real laughter, a feeling of joy sprung suddenly from deep inside him, coming up past the cereal all along his chest and throat.

"Stop," Gary says, but Jim loves this feeling, soaring inside.

"This is the manic part," Gary says. "You have to say no to this."

The idea of saying no only increases the joy. Jim can hardly breathe.

"It's just as important to stop the euphoria as it is to stop the depression," Gary says. "You have to even off."

Jim imagines himself some rough blob getting both ends sawn off. He feels so much better, lighter, insane the relief and how complete it can be. He can imagine never being in pain again. "You're killing me," he says, and this makes him laugh harder. Words the strangest of all.

"Please," Gary says, and Jim feels instantly guilty, even in his joy, and then rage, so quickly.

"Fuck you," Jim says. "That's exactly what I mean. I can't even laugh without it being something bad I've done to my family, and I have to feel guilty. For two fucking seconds of laughter. Because we're not allowed that, not even that. That's what family is."

"Jesus."

"We've had enough of Jesus. Mary sucking his dick all day long and you letting her."

Gary swings from across the table but this time Jim raises his arm and blocks it, throws his cereal bowl in Gary's face, impact and milk and cereal everywhere, the two of them rising in what has happened in every mead hall since there were mead halls, locked in battle, Gary tackling him hard but he somehow gets free, sees the enormous plate of glass looking over the valley and runs straight for it to break through and soar thirty feet to the ground but everything will be denied him, the glass so damn strong he only folds against it, painful, something happening to his shoulder and knee, and he bounces off and is back on the carpet and doesn't want to move again. Closes his eyes and refuses to be here, too many indignities all at once.

"Fucking psycho," Gary says.

It's a long drive to Lakeport, more than two hours. Wine country, vineyards sprung up along the highway north of Santa Rosa. Small redneck towns transforming into boutiques. Not complete yet, old shacks and beaters remaining next to the mansions and Porsches, but all Jim knew is being erased, the pear orchards and apples, old pickup trucks and gun racks and bowling and diners.

Cloverdale is a holdout, though. Same crappy shops and houses interrupting the highway, all traffic forced to crawl through. The reassuring feeling of nothing happening, meaningless lives still plodding along small and predictable, the sawmill still here and all the industrial supplies and no sign of progress.

They stop at Fosters Freeze, as they always have. This is where Elizabeth handed off the kids to him every weekend when he was still living in Lakeport. The halfway point. He's had the chocolate chip shake a million times, just that chocolate coating blended with vanilla ice cream and a bit of milk, big clumps of chocolate always left in the bottom. And corn dogs, two each.

"Their bounty was unmeasured," Jim says. "Foods from many lands, the most exotic spices."

"Yeah, that's the way I think of a corn dog."

"We have the same thoughts these days, brother. We've never been closer."

"Yeah. How's your shoulder after running into the window?"

"The crease mark will be there for a while."

"I can't even think of the dumb shit you might do. Running into the window. What the fuck was that?"

"I was going to fly."

"Well that's not going to work."

"Good to know."

"We shouldn't be eating here. Mom's fixing venison for lunch."

"I wanted to see this place one last time. Where I picked up my kids every weekend, one of the signs of how my life went."

"It's not gone. It's still here."

"I feel like I'm looking back on it already. Maybe that's the afterlife, just pure nostalgia, neither good nor bad. No heaven or hell, just some tug from what was."

"Enough."

"You're not curious?"

"No."

Jim examines his corn dog, the layers in the pressed meat. It could be peeled like an onion or calve like a glacier. And somehow this dog has become loose in its shell, a gap developed all around and the shiny smooth walls of the corn exposed, subterranean. "Look what the corn does to the light," he says. "Cave adventure. We could sell tickets."

"Fuck," Gary says.

"What?"

But Gary just shakes his head and stares into the parking lot.

Each part was intolerable. The marriage or the divorce, having a family or being separated from his kids, working or not working, his parents and brother close or far. And every decision limited to the options available. When was there ever a choice?

His shake is close to the end and his gut overfull with that sick feeling of sugar overdose. The promised chunks of chocolate at the bottom, like scabs with their odd rough shapes formed when lava hit cold. Scalloped edges broken by the beaters. "I really am looking back already. I know I will never see this shake again. Last time. It's not a what if. I'm already gone."

"Just hold it together for a quick visit with the parents. Two nights in Lakeport and then we'll be back down to see the therapist again."

"You don't know how long two nights are."

"Yeah, because I've never lived a day and night. Only you have done that."

"That's right. A night without being immersed. A night not in your life. You haven't had that yet."

"Neither have you. No one can have that."

"Mysteries of despair. Whole new lands opening up, just like the cavern in this corn dog. You may visit these lands someday yourself."

"I won't."

"How do you know?"

"Same as knowing things fall down not up. Or knowing the ground is made of dirt."

"I'm jealous."

"No you're not. You've always looked down on me. Not an A student like you."

"I mean it. I'm jealous in every way possible."

"Well let's hit the road," Gary says, and with that they rise and dump their trash and climb aboard. As they pull onto the road Jim is still thinking of the trash can with all its smears of ice cream and chocolate, everyone ordering exactly what he ordered, the cream gone thick and yellow in previous sun.

They're out of town quickly, passing the sawmill with its piles of pulp and angled conveyors and rising into hills so green at this time of year, all the sugar pines settled on new grass and even the oaks budding new leaves, springtime already and only March. Winter just finding its depth in Fairbanks.

Old railroad tracks rarely used now, the highway cut along the river, Jim craning for a look at the water to see the level but the gorge is fairly deep in most places and he gets only glimpses. Lover's leap, one of many in California, a common thing among earlier natives to go soaring off a cliff whenever love went wrong.

"They had something there," Jim says.

"What?"

"Jumping off the cliff. Does make a statement about how the whole thing feels."

"That's just a legend. Probably no one's ever done it."

"I bet a hundred have done it, right there. So high above the water, exposed rock, really beautiful. You'd want it to be there."

"So you can see the past now."

"Yeah. Our Cherokee blood. Allows me to have visions of the ancestors. And just think how far they go back. Maybe ten thousand years."

"Please none of this horseshit with Mom and Dad. They're worried. They might believe you actually have visions. For some reason they've always just believed anything you say."

"Really?"

"Yeah, and nothing I say. I hate it."

"Wow. I had no idea."

"Yeah. The world outside your head. Surprise."

"I'm sorry," Jim says. "I really am sorry for being oblivious to so much. But of course no one can ever do anything about not noticing. They didn't notice."

"It's okay. I really don't mind. I just want you to get well now."

"Thank you."

They take the turnoff for going over Hopland, just before the bridge. Narrow road and the feeling of lift on the dips. Small vineyards and then a town of maybe fifty people where they've always had a speed trap. Crawling along at twenty-five and still it takes only a minute to get through town.

"Small towns," Jim says. "Not one of us has ever tried a city. I wonder what that would have been like."

"Awful. Too many people. Can't even park your car."

"But think about who we became. We supported Nixon. Without a thought but just because everyone else from our town did too. And you actually put down 'uprisings' as you called them, beating up Indians at school before finding out we're part Cherokee, and Dad said nothing about that at the time."

"That has nothing to do with city or small town."

"But it does. We own guns, and the only vacation we ever took as a family was to hunt or fish. All our spare time spent killing. The people who live in cities don't do that."

"Who cares?"

"This all matters. All this is part of my suicide."

"There is no suicide."

"But there is, coming soon, and I just want to understand it first. I want to know why when I pull the trigger."

"Goddammit."

"Yeah. Why let me talk. And why think. Better just to drive fast for a while."

They're winding now into hills, tight switchbacks and Gary going too fast, accelerating so much he has to brake at each curve even though they're climbing. Throaty sound of the engine.

"Punch it," Jim says. "Hard as you can. See if we can fly off one of these drops. Easier for the parents that way, even though they lose two sons instead of one. Too much shame in suicide."

Gary gone silent again, clutching the wheel and not slowing down. Some of the drops are fairly sheer and onto rocks and would do the trick. Others they'd just get caught in the trees.

"I guess our best chance is from a head-on," Jim says. "Someone coming fast down the hill. Otherwise the chances actually seem pretty slim."

It feels like they're crossing over to something more, not just over the mountain to Lakeport. Gary a ferryman taking him across the river to hell, but even that's too simple. Gary wanting him well and thinking these visits and crossing miles will help, that the gaps in Jim's mind can be traversed externally. But for Jim it's all more like sitting in a waiting room.

"There's no rush," he says to Gary. "We're not getting anywhere, and we're no further away from my future."

Thin canyons forested but the wider, drier hillsides are covered in short brush that looks bluish in overcast light. Scanning for bucks out of habit. The road widens toward the top and Gary goes even faster until they summit and see the other side, Clearlake stretched out with hills all around. Largest natural lake in California.

"Stop for the view?" Jim asks, but Gary is concentrated, having to brake hard now on the downhill hairpins and still stomping the accelerator anyway.

"It's nice I won't have to kill myself," Jim says. "Thanks for being willing to go with me. It won't be bad on the other side. I promise. Just nothing and more of nothing, which is better than the minus we have now."

The lake always looks like it's sitting too low, the mountains on the far shore higher and bending toward the water making a sort of crease that pushes everything down, the whole valley under pressure. But the view doesn't last long, especially at this speed. They descend into the prettiest small vales, all pale green ghost pines in here, sparse and plenty of open space between. Idyllic hillsides that make you want to hold a rifle or shotgun low in one hand and just hike for hours, crossing the easiest terrain. The ground scabbed with small outcrops of black rock crumbling or the smoother gray stone. Flecks of red and green everywhere and the occasional Lake County diamond or arrowhead but all of it so easy your boots leave almost no mark and you don't have to scrape through brush. Small streams you can hop across. Gray squirrels taking flight, their tails in arcs, and the rough call of jays. Jim could hike here forever.

Then the flats and Gary accelerates, lofting over rises, the truck feeling like something too heavy being dragged along by an asthmatic engine.

"Your truck isn't going to make it," Jim says. "We'll be walking the last part."

But Gary of course says nothing. "Buddha Gary," Jim says. "What worlds inside his head."

A long straightaway before the highway, a few houses widely spaced, and Gary opens it up, the needle pushing past a hundred. Jim feels a thrill, rolls down his window to get the blast of cold air. Sticks his arm out and bangs on the side of his door, like when they see a buck, hoots and hollers at the hills and random folk hidden away in their cozy homes.

But Gary has to slow around the bend and stop at the light for the highway, speed and thrill so quickly gone, and then they cross and crawl through town, new businesses at this end but then everything familiar.

"So small," Jim says. "So fucking small. Seriously a one-street town, called Main Street in a burst of imagination. The other side streets are only for houses and go nowhere."

Through the center and glimpses of the lake, the park, a left hook and on to the most familiar stretch with his former dental practice right across the street from Safeway, where he worked all through high school. A kind of joke to make him work his whole life within a few hundred yards. Prisons we don't even see. God's plan, each with our own invisible thumb pressing us down. "Sky thumbs," Jim says. "I've had a vision. Let me tell you what god is, little brother."

"Almost there," Gary says. "Can it. You can be crazy with me, but don't do that to Mom and Dad."

"Yes sir."

Houses along the water and their own coming into view, long narrow lot with hedge and lawn out front, the small sturdy white house with its bay window for breakfast, where his father always sits and is sitting now, fat blank face staring at the lake.

They roll in the driveway along pansies and petunias his mother plants constantly, and the pomegranate tree. Side entrance up red concrete steps. Large two-story garage ahead where a hundred antlers are stored, hung in the rafters. The house and the garage places that refuse to be only that, storing too much time and memory.

"I feel like my brain is going to break from all the memories here," Jim says.

"Nothing like that," Gary says. "Say nothing like that to them. I mean it."

"What do I say then?"

"I don't know. Say it was good to see your kids. Talk about what Fairbanks is like now. Just play pinochle and talk about our usual whatever."

"Well that all sounds solid. Should get me through a couple minutes."

"Time isn't this thing you have to get through. It's nothing. Just live your life."

"But that's the whole thing. Right there."

"Just can it. Seriously."

"Yeah, you should be a therapist."

"No thanks."

"What a loss to the world of therapy."

Gary is up the steps and has opened the creaky screen door. Not one of them ever bothering to give it a bit of oil over the last forty years. It made the same sound when Jim was a kid.

Pavement uneven beneath him, cracks and the steps threatening to shear off. Ants everywhere, even in winter. His memories of them are only in summer.

The small entryway, like a pantry off the kitchen painted yellow and never used for anything. Then the green beans on the stove in a pot, where they've been cooking for hours or days. Just beans and water, no effort at flavor, sodden mush that could be swallowed without chewing. Direct nutrition. The same stainless steel pots from his childhood, same stovetop, nothing ever changing here. Same dark green linoleum, all overwhelming. Long narrow kitchen with his father sat at the end in the bay window and his mother at her station at the sink, hands resting on a dish towel.

"Hi Mom," Jim says, because it's silent and they all seem to be waiting.

"Well," she says.

"Yeah," he says. "That about sums it up."

Her lips tight, worried, and so many wrinkles now in her face. His own mother grown old. And so he's been here long enough. It's not early, really. Thirty-nine was old in earlier times.

"How have you been, Mom?" he asks, making an effort, and her lips open a bit, her head tilting to the side in worry and love.

"Oh we're fine," she says. "Busy with the church. Easter."

He doesn't know what to say in response to that. What do you say to nothing?

"Wow," he finally says. "Preparing early."

She's wearing a blue floral pattern, something she's had for decades now. You could call it a shirt except it's too thick and goes too low and has a kind of ruffled collar, almost like in Shakespeare's time.

"What do you call that kind of shirt?" he asks.

She clutches at the fabric between her breasts with one hand and looks worried. "Just a blouse I guess," she says.

"You've had it for so long."

"Yes."

"I think my head is going to split from how nothing has changed here. I could be fifteen years old and everything looks the same. You look old now, and you're bigger, and you have that loose neck, but otherwise you could be the same. You have the same hairdo as then, seriously the same hairdo you had in 1955."

"Jim!" She says it in her sharp way to discipline. Leaning back slightly, as if trying to see him from a distance.

"Sorry," Jim says, and he wonders why Gary has said nothing, not stepping in to tackle him or shut him up. His father is watching, fat hangdog cheeks and bald head, only tufts of white on the sides, sun spots and red-brown skin. Hands hanging, one over the back of the seat and the other off the edge of the table, thick fingers like potato wedges sat too long in the display. "Well?" Jim asks. "Anything to say, Dad?"

"You don't talk like that," his father says.

"Yeah," Jim says. "Yeah. And what was the point of that?"

"We stopped in Cloverdale on the way," Gary says. "Had a corn dog, but we should still be hungry enough for lunch. It was a while ago."

"Well good," his mother says. "Go take a seat at the dining table and I'll serve the food."

"And Dad, you're wearing the same thing." A zippered thin green sweater, but not loose knit. Made for hunting, a bit of camo. "I don't know what that's called either. It's not a sweater, not a jacket, not a vest. What do you call that?"

"That's enough," his father says.

"Have you been fat that long? When did it first happen? Because I remember you stretching whatever that is since I was a kid. And is it really the same one, or did you just buy the same thing over and over?"

Gary has a hand on his arm now. Another wrestling match is necessary, apparently, right here in the kitchen tossed in with the overcooked green beans and the hidden stock of a hundred worn green hunting sweaters and a hundred blue floral blouses burying them until they'll disappear into the sinkhole that's opening up right here. Jim can see himself falling through eternity wrapped in the clothing of his parents, a kind of birth vision, arms and legs ruffling.

But Gary doesn't do more. Just holds his arm, and somehow that has stopped Jim at least for the moment, because of the vision.

"Camo in the kitchen," Jim says. "Because you wouldn't want anyone to see you here. Have to remain invisible."

And his father does that, on cue. Doesn't say a thing or change his expression, which is of nothing, bovine.

"Cud," Jim says. "All cud. This house, this life and family and all our years. I would shoot you just to get a reaction."

"Jim!" his mother says.

"Sorry," he says. "You're right. Everything is fine. It really was fine. Empty but that's okay. I don't know why it stopped being okay."

"It's just the pain in your head," his mother says.

"Yeah. And more than that."

"Just the pain in your head," she says. "You need to get sinus surgery or better medication, or some pills for your mood, something. It's just a chemical imbalance."

The earnest look on her face, believing all this and wanting to help. Isn't our mother going to be the last person we think of, right at the end, however we end? Why isn't it in her power to do more? Why can't family stop anything or reach anything? "I wish you could do more," Jim says. "I wish you could help. I need help. I really do. I can't find my way back, and I don't know what happened."

"We're here to help you," Gary says.

"Like the trees."

"What?"

"The trees want to help too. They're trying their best. Just can't talk and don't have arms and can't go anywhere because they don't have legs. But they're doing what they can."

"It's just the pain," his mother says. "Can't they give you something for that?"

"I'm on pills now for depression or whatever. The roller coaster. Trying to re-lay tracks on flat ground. A coaster that just goes round and round but you don't need any restraining bar because it's not going to do a loop or roll or climb."

"How can the doctor talk like that?"

"He didn't. He just said the pills will make everything worse for two weeks, and good luck to you pilgrim."

"None of this makes sense," she says.

"That's right."

"You were always so bright, and so happy."

"I wasn't happy."

"Yes you were."

"Okay. I was happy all the time."

"Don't do that."

"Do what?"

"Talk like that."

"You mean agree with you?"

"This isn't you."

"It's all that's left, whatever it is. What else could be called me?"

She looks down, turns back to the sink, folds a small dish towel and then smooths it, over and over, with one palm and then another. Floral pattern again, but pink, small imaginary flowers, more perfect than real ones but faded from so many washings. Her mouth open just a bit.

"You look so worried," he says.

"Well I am."

Her breath slow and labored, her whole body tense. Her chin a kind of loose bulb but even that looks tense.

"I'm sorry," he says. "None of this is something I'm trying to do to any of you."

"Well we should have lunch," she says. "Before the venison is cold. You can carry the platter to the table."

So Jim lifts the yellowed ceramic platter with its pilings of venison breaded and fried, dark crumbed shards. Simple food but good, and he's ready to try. Just sit and eat and chat about nothing and think nothing.

The dining room so small and carpeted, low ceilinged and dark, one curtained window looking out to the lake. Sideboard with glossy plates and cutlery, a tray of photos and knickknacks in front of the window, too many things loading this place. Small bedside table holding a thick yellow phone book and the old green phone. A step down to the living room through an archway. California architecture, small but with archways after the stars.

"Looks good, Mom," Gary is saying, and Jim has somehow already sat and has a piece of venison on his plate. He missed a few moments of transition, not sure where they went. He wants to agree but can't say anything, only nods his head.

Green beans wet and exhausted beside the meat, and scalloped potatoes thick with cheese.

"Dear Lord," his mother says, her hands clasped together in prayer. "Thank you for this food and our family joined together, and please help my boy Jim. Help guide him and comfort him and make your love clear. Help get us all through this difficult time. Please Lord, and thank you. Amen."

"Amen," Gary says. Jim and his father remain silent. Jim hasn't thought even to fold his hands.

"Do you believe, Dad?" Jim asks. "Did you ever believe?"

"You don't ask that question," his mother says.

"I want to know, Dad."

"Let's eat," his father says.

"Do you believe in god. Did you ever believe in god. That's what I'm asking."

"I know what you're asking."

"Well then?"

"Because you have a problem doesn't mean I have a problem."

"But I come from you."

"A long time ago."

"You made me. And I want to know what made me. Where do I get this feeling that I'm a piece of shit? Is it from you or is it from Mom?"

"Jim," his mother says. "You were in the church all your life."

"That's what I mean."

"Well you make it sound like it was bad, like we hurt you."

"That's what I'm saying."

"You need to take some responsibility," Gary says. "You made your own choices. Cheating on your wife. Divorce. Rhoda. Living on your own. Not seeing your family. And even not going to church. Your choice, as I said yesterday. I don't go to church, and I don't feel guilty about it."

They're all still cutting pieces of venison to eat. Somehow the meal is still happening, knives and forks working. He can taste the butter. Fried in butter, everything they eat, with these same breadcrumbs. Catfish, crappie, bluegill, steelhead, venison. Only the birds are cooked differently, basically just stuck in the oven plain.

Jim chews and chews, rubbery and gamey, blood in the butter, and finally swallows. "You're right," he says. "It is my fault. I guess that's the problem. Somehow the fact that I destroyed my own life makes me feel sorry for myself, and that's even more dangerous, the self-pity. I don't know how it works or how to stop it. I want it to be someone else's fault because then I'd be fighting on my side at least and might get somewhere."

"How can you talk like that?" his mother asks. "That doesn't even make sense."

"It does. If I can't fight for me there's no way out. And for some reason I haven't been able to for a long time."

"All you have to do is stop."

"That's what Gary says."

"Well he's right."

"Shut up for just a sec. I'm thinking. I feel like I'm close to something."

"Telling your mother to shut up," his father says. "You leave now."

"Stop being small for just a minute. Just shut up and let me think." Jim is barely holding on to some recognition, something true about how he might find a way to fight for himself, some spatial sense of that riding alongside his current self, only an arm's length away, something he can almost touch.

"Leave!" his father yells, and this is so rare, so unbelievably rare for him to raise his voice, to respond or care about anything, all they can do is stare at him, all of them.

"It's you, Dad," Jim says. "You're finally here. Welcome to the family. We last saw you about thirty years ago."

His father rises and comes around the table faster than Jim would have thought possible, more nimble, a fist grabbing the back of Jim's collar, knuckles against his spine, hoisting. He doesn't resist, finds his legs under him and is marched through the kitchen out the screen door and down the cracked concrete steps and still that fist pushing him forward along the driveway toward the road. So hot here in summer, baking, so many years of memories of this concrete, cold and wet now, and his father stops the moment Jim's boots hit the dirt and gravel portion.

His father lets go and walks over to the gate, swings it closed now, a gate wide enough for the whole driveway, never used, and Jim had in fact forgotten about it. But now he's on the other side. The gate blocking him from the driveway, and the hedge blocking him from the lawn. A small no-man's-land before the road. He never realized until now that this small turnaround area was not part of the home. Anytime he played here as a kid he was in foreign territory without even knowing it and could have been lost.

His father has not paused for conversation but has gone back inside. No surprises there.

So Jim traverses the no-man's-land and then the road, not even looking for traffic, not caring, but of course is not run over, and when he reaches the other side he wants to continue to the lake, the small beach and tules, but a wire fence has been put up by the association just recently for insurance concerns. Someone might fall or drown and sue the local homeowners, because that all makes sense. So he climbs the fence, feeling like a convict on escape day, struggles at the top because the toes of his boots are too big and rounded to get any grip in the links. And the wire thin and hard on his hands. But he gets his legs over and jumps down. One hand catches a bit and he can imagine a finger popping off but it stays intact for now.

Chunks of concrete here before the beach, and maybe that was the concern. His son has a long scar on one shin from them.

So much litter along the water's edge, blue and red soda cans and white Styrofoam making a kind of flag in the tules, and the stink of green scum and rot, bloated dead carp. The lake was always putrid at the edges but the water itself was clear. Now huge mats of algae are clogging it up and turning it all green even in winter.

He makes divots in the rough sand, what there is of it, remembers a beach and swimming, but how could he ever have thought of this as a beach? He shot ducks from right here back when there were ducks and it was legal. He remembers the spray for mosquitoes, also, all the poison spread on the water. Remembers waves, very rare, and flooding over the road and lawn and up the first two concrete steps to the house. Remembers how brown the water was then. Remembers kissing Jane Williams right here, standing in this same place how many years ago on a summer night, trying to feel under her bra, because hunks of fat are everything.

The water farther out, with the light reflected, looks cold, one of a thousand shades of gray that water and sky can do. This day not the same as any other, resistant. It won't be shaped by his memories. And he has no idea what to do. Stand here or go back inside or walk somewhere else and leave. How is he supposed to decide?

All he can think of is Rhoda. Whenever there's a moment not filled with something else she comes flooding in, unstoppable. The ache for her. She's somewhere in Lake-port. She's purposely not told him where, but he can find her. He knows where her sisters and brother live, every one of their houses, knows the restaurant they own, the pool company, knows where they eat and drink. No one can hide in this town.

So he climbs the fence again, wire digging into the back of his leg when he straddles the top, and jumps down onto the safe side. The horrors and dangers of the waterfront escaped, the homeowners breathing their collective sigh. He'd like to slip a giant butter knife under the town, just at the water's edge, and then flip the whole thing into the lake.

The driveway gate is not locked so he swings it back to the pansies. Resistance is futile. He is the unstoppable Jim, Giant Jim, riding a new and improved euphoria, euphoria with purpose.

He gets in the truck, where Gary has left his keys in the ignition, one more sign of growing up in a small town, and backs down the drive in a sober fashion, slowly, so as not to alarm anyone. They should be running out of the house now and stopping him, but of course that isn't happening. His father sitting in the window again, gazing expressionless, Jim in his passing no different than clouds in the sky.

He backs into the street without even looking, willing the quick end, disappointed as always, and drives toward the center of town. The diner Rhoda's sister and brother-in-law own, a good place to start. Except that then she will be alerted. He takes the bend to Safeway and his dental office and pulls into the parking lot. He needs a plan. Here is where Rhoda worked for him, where they first met, where they first fucked. A sacred place of origin, capable of pointing the way. A depressing little brown building, a woman emerging now with her son after a bit of torture. Causing pain every day. It's supposed to be one of the reasons dentists have the highest suicide rate, swapping every year or so with psychiatrists, who are obviously fucked. Otherwise why would they be in that profession? But the dental suicides are a little more mysterious maybe.

"What to do," Jim says aloud. "What to do."

The most likely would be her sister Donna's place, big and with extra rooms. Donna's the one closest to Rhoda. But Rhoda may have rented her own place now, in which case his chances will be small.

"Have to start somewhere," he says. He pulls out of the parking lot and turns away from the water. Donna and her husband, Jim, live in the hills at the edge of town. They have a small diner and have mortgaged everything as heavily as possible to pretend to be kings. But why not. At least they want something. Jim would like to want something simple like a house. He has a brand-new one in Fairbanks, no furniture yet even, and honestly doesn't give a shit. Two stories of nothing, specially built fireplace where no one will gather, enormous empty hearth, some external shell he built to remind himself exactly how lonely he is. He'd rather live anywhere else now. Lost in the paper birch, endless, no neighbor in sight. Even the trees thin.

Road with no sidewalk, houses with no lawns, only untrimmed grass and weeds growing, everything taking a dump as you get farther from the water. Then a couple exits on the highway and turning up a new road cut into hillside that hasn't been braced and will be falling down soon. Small twisted black oak out here, and manzanita, the kinds of low hills all around Lakeport, and houses widely spaced.

He turns into their gravel drive. A new gray house, two stories, probably four or five thousand square feet, ridiculous, with deck and hot tub and gazebo out back. Three other cars but none he recognizes. He doesn't know what she's driving now.

The pickup engine collapses with a rattle and he waits a bit, rolls down the window. Scrub jays calling, rough and unapologetic. Flight of one of them in that long swoop upward before landing.

He reaches behind the seat for his valise and the magnum, lifts it out heavy and cold and looks at it in his lap, considering. Turns it over a few times. Then he reaches for the shells, so blunt and wide. Squared-off gray ends, heavy lead. He opens the cylinder and inserts them one at a time.

He steps out and tucks the pistol into the back of his jeans under his jacket. Long barrel and so heavy. He may accidentally shoot off his own ass, which would be kind of funny. Always had a small ass but there's always more to lose. He can feel himself grinning.

"Joker," he says. "Flat-ass Jim. No-ass Jim. Here for a reckoning. I want my ass back."

No-ass Jim saunters toward the house like any corral. Hear you're hiding my woman here. He should say something like that. Bring her out before I burn this place to the ground.

The front steps are terra-cotta, which must be slippery as fuck in the rain. He mounts carefully. The ground everywhere still wet.

The knocker is a pig snout, which seems appropriate for the gluttony of such a big house. Gourmands inside just finishing up some pâté not knowing they're about to enter a western. Wrong set, wrong time.

Jim comes to the door. Two Jims. "Hi Jim," Jim says, and "Hi Jim," Jim says back. He looks like Elvis, full head of dark hair, not receding, and long sideburns. A bit pudgy, but a handsome man. One of the town's bourgeois leaders, a business owner, the kind of person with something to lose when the stranger comes to town, the kind of person laws are meant to protect. Whereas No-ass Jim is more a desperado at this point.

"I want my ass back," he says.

"What?"

"I'm thinking I have a flat ass, or no ass, so I want it back." Jim smiles. "Well let's take a look and see if we can help. Maybe a steady diet of pancakes down at the diner. It's been working for me." Jim rubs his belly. Wearing a polo shirt with horizontal stripes, not fitting into a western at all.

"Can't," No-ass Jim says. "Hiding something back there." Jim grins again. "Aren't we all."

"So is Rhoda here? I won't cause any problems. She's been helping me out, talking with me on the phone to help me get through the day, so I guess I could just call her, but I'm never alone, and I don't want to have that talk in front of my brother or parents. I'd like to just see her now in person."

"She's not here, Jim. I'm sorry." He looks like he's lying. No-ass thinks about pulling the pistol to be a bit more insistent, but if she's really not here that would end everything. Police would be called and No-ass would no longer be free to pull his horse up to whatever hitching post he wants.

"Okay. Not sure I believe you."

"Well you can take a look. Come inside and walk through every room. Be my guest. She's not here." The Jim who belongs spreads his arm wide to invite into the realm. If he's lying, this is a good ploy. Pretty convincing.

"Okay. I'll go look for my ass elsewhere then I guess."

"Okay."

"Okay. Happy Easter. Where is she? Where can I find her?"

"You know I'm not supposed to say."

"Yeah, and you'll be calling her now to warn her, right?"

"Yeah, of course. I have to."

"Okay. See you later."

"Bye, Jim. And good luck to you. I hope you feel better."

No-ass turns around and walks with big steps to the truck, tired of being a pity case. It never feels good when people feel sorry for you. And who is this other Jim anyway? No-ass was valedictorian. What happened?

He backs the truck calmly then spins the wheel and peels out, fishtailing down the road and keeping the accelerator pinned, the engine choking on itself and the trees moving faster. Then he punches the brakes and fishtails again, bed of the truck so far to the right he almost flips. The feel of that point approaching. But he slides in the thin layer of gravel mysteriously left on top of the asphalt and comes to a stop, sideways in the road. No one else around. Smell of his tires. He rolls down a window and feels the cool air, smells the engine. Old oil mixing with fried rubber. The sky so gray and empty.

He just doesn't know what to do. Leave the truck and walk into the hills? Drive to some other place she might be? Go back to his parents' house? Drive to Santa Rosa to see his kids again? Go to Mexico?

He gets out of the truck for some fresh air and to clear his head. Leaves it sideways in the road and door open, like an accident or a crime scene. If someone comes, let them have questions. Jim has questions too.

The grass is wet and long here, no grazing. The stunted black oaks not blocking any sun, everything around them grown wild. Big stands of poison oak, waxy. So many fallen sticks, his boots crunching with every step. Oak balls dark brown and slimy, rotting. Spiderwebs everywhere. He has to keep brushing them aside.

So much lichen on everything, rock and tree, in white and black lace. No surface clean. And the dream of walking forever isn't possible because every ten feet is such a hassle, never in a direct line, always having to sidetrack around some bit of brush or deadfall. It feels like a job.

Jim turns around, crunches back through all the sticks, peels away spiderwebs, tries not to slip on the rot, and is standing at the truck again. At least the options have narrowed by one.

He'll try Sandra's house. She's the black sheep of the family, a good place to hide. And not far away.

Down the highway a couple stops and into the back side of town, quiet lanes of trash and untrimmed weeds but pretty enough, peaceful. A small house hunched on a mound elevated maybe ten feet above the road, mini hill for a mini kingdom. Two thin tracks of concrete for a driveway, accommodating the wheels only, grass between grown long enough to brush the underside.

Nose of the pickup pointing upward when he stops. He tucks the magnum behind his back and walks to the front porch, sagging thin wood and cracked gray paint. Raps on the door and steps back.

He has to wait, and then the door opens slowly. Sandra with long dark hair, only a girl still, maybe twenty or twenty-one, because Rhoda is ten years younger than him and Sandra almost ten years younger than that.

"How did you get a house?" he asks. "You're so young. I just realized."

"Benefits of the pool empire," she says.

"I guess the empire is over now."

"Yeah, Mom killing Dad will do that."

"Sorry."

"Not your fault. At least not that we know. Were you having an affair with my Dad too?"

"No. Not that I know of. Unless he got me when I was sleeping over there."

"He wasn't above that."

"Wow."

"Yeah. So why are you here, Jim?"

"Direct just like your sister."

"Like our mom."

"Okay. Well I want to see Rhoda."

"Off limits."

"Why though?"

"Because you're suicidal and crazy desperate and a dipshit for cheating on her? Does that ring any bells?"

"I guess so. But there are other ways to look at it."

"Such as?"

"Maybe I loved as well as I could. Maybe this is the best me I'm offering, and that's all anyone can do."

"Not good enough."

"You're young but mean."

"We haven't even started."

"Well. Is she here?"

"No."

"Would you tell me if she was?"

"No."

"So she might be here."

"No. She actually isn't."

Jim feels like he's talking to Rhoda. It's the same raw directness he likes, and she's slimmer the way Rhoda used to be, same dark hair and small face. Not beautiful in a way everyone would agree on, but some witchiness he likes. And her top just a black stretch thing with a low cutaway showing cleavage. Where he's looking now.

"Maybe you should go," she says.

"Or stay. I could stay."

"Stay and do what?"

"A fresh start. Maybe you and me instead of me and Rhoda. A newer better version of us, clean and without any history."

"Do you want me to puke right here on your shoes, or should I run for the sink?"

"Don't be mean."

"Honestly I would puke."

"That's not kind."

"Out of control, Jim. You need to slow down. Stop looking outside. And leave my sister alone. She's already got enough of her own problems. There was our parents, yeah? And the whole fight over the estate? And trying things now with Rich? Maybe give her a chance."

"In theory that sounds good."

"Try doing it."

"The weather again."

"What?"

"Snap my fingers and blow out the sun."

"You mean you can't control your feelings?"

"Bingo."

She leans her cheek against the edge of the door. "I can see you're not actually a bad guy. Just pathetic. But leave her alone, yeah? Don't ever try to see her or talk to her again. You had your chances."

"We need more than that. Everyone needs more than that." He thinks about the magnum. Again it might be useful. And his mind is working in new ways. What had seemed like crime before doesn't seem like crime now. He could force her to be with him, and would that really be wrong? He reaches back, his hand closing on the grip, so certain, the gun a maker of law, a maker of new right and wrong. But it will be used one time only. He knows that. Because no one will agree with this new law. So he needs to save it still, until he finds Rhoda.

"What about money?" he asks. "What if I paid you a thousand dollars to be with me right now?"

Her face looks so disgusted, really like she might vomit, and she closes the door. He knocks, but he knows she's not going to answer. He could break it in, but again he's not ready for the end yet. And what has he missed? She's smart, and she knows Rhoda well. He might have discovered more here in this conversation, if he'd been able to keep sex out of it. But he's never been able to do that. Sex and despair the same thing, both limiting what the world will be, both irresistible.

He tries the diner next. Not really hungry after the corn dogs and venison, but he orders a stack of pancakes with bacon. Donna is the soft one, large and matronly, always kind. "How are you, Jim?" she asks, and there's room left for him to answer.

"You're really asking," he says.

"Yes."

"I like that. Why is Rhoda's family so much better than mine?"

She chuckles, soft and friendly. "You haven't been to any of our meetings about the estate. We're the worst family you could imagine."

"But even when you say that, you seem so nice it's hard to believe."

"I'm one of the ones cutting Rhoda out of the will. My own closest sister. Because we need the money for our new house. We went too far. The mortgage is too big."

"How could you do that to her?"

"Mom always hated Rhoda, because she was too much like her. So I'm just following her wishes. I'm not doing anything to mend the situation and make it fair. If I were a good person, I would want it to be fair, but I'm not. I can see now I'm like everyone else."

"Rhoda's not like that."

"True. She's actually generous and fundamentally doesn't care about money. I know she'll still love me and talk to me even after I screw her in the estate."

"Wow."

"Yeah. But back to the question. How are you?"

Jim is looking around at this place, a basic diner, nothing fancy, big plates of eggs and potatoes and pancakes, all-day breakfast mixed in with turkey dinners and minestrone soup for late lunch or an afternoon snack, almost all the customers obese and wearing crap jackets over T-shirts, most of the men in baseball caps. He never belonged here. "About me," he says. "Maybe I'm going to kill myself soon, very soon. Who knows? I don't know when it started or when it will end. But I need to see Rhoda again. You have to help me see her."

Donna sets down the plates she's been holding, the remains of someone else's lunch. She looks so much more tired suddenly. "Don't do that to her, Jim," she says. "You don't know what it's like after a suicide, when it's someone who was close. You could break her with that. Even Rhoda. Strongest person I know, but if you add that right after she's been through this, less than a year later, I think that's too much. You can't do it."

"It's not a thing I can make a decision about. I'm just reporting to you the way things are going, not saying I want them to go that way."

"You know that's not true. You're making a decision, even now. When my dad was running away, my mom didn't have to raise the shotgun and fire. She could have let him go. She had already written a suicide note to him."

"I think she pulled the trigger without a thought, without a single thought."

"It was a choice."

"What if she was only watching at that point? No longer living her life but only watching it happen? Momentum. Everything set in motion."

"Don't believe that. It's dangerous to believe that."

"But think about what was happening in your mother's life. The marriage over, against her will, no choice at all about it, and he'd just told her he'd had an affair for the last sixteen years, right?"

"Yes."

"And he said all those years were a lie, as if she didn't live them. Sixteen years gone, and the worth of all the married years before that. Maybe that's too much to lose."

"That's true, but she still didn't have to kill him."

"I think she did, and just because he had a big gun collection. That simple. The guns were there, and everything in her life was not possible, and that's when a gun bridges the gap. The gun brings the pieces back together. It's like a power to bend time and event, the only thing that can fight momentum. The world can make sense again. And more than that, she can become real again. After she pulls the trigger, she reenters her life. She's present again, and that's what she had lost."

"You're dangerous, Jim. Don't you see my sister."

"But I have to see her."

"Don't you do it. Don't you take her from me, you asshole." Donna has grabbed his upper arm now, shaking it, and he realizes she's so big and her arms as strong as his.

"Do you have a gun?" she asks.

"No," he says, and he's trying to free his arm but she's holding on and they're both standing now, and people are looking. "I don't have it. I'm seeing a therapist, and they made me stay away."

"Well you stay away. That's right. You stay away from all of us. Go back to Alaska and do whatever you want up there."

She's pulling him toward the door, the second time today he's been forced to leave. Apparently he's not getting along with anyone too well. "My pancakes," he says.

"You leave her alone, Jim," she says, and he can feel her shaking as she pushes him out the door and the small bells jingle and she closes it after him fast and locks it. Only glass, and he has the pistol and could shoot her right now through the glass and shoot some of the good folk eating their pancakes, too, but he feels too tired. So tired and so low, crashing fast, and he just sits on the edge of one of the huge ceramic pots holding flowers. A bit of sun coming through the clouds, bright overcast, and no one driving or walking on this street knows anything about him or what was just said, all reset again, waiting for the new Jim to re-form.

He drives back to his parents. He will call Rhoda, because he's not going to find her. She's been hidden away. They saw him coming, the whole town boarded up, only dust and sun, the sheriff waiting on a rocking chair on a wooden porch or maybe even he has been locked inside. The saloon doors free to swing but no one in there except a bartender hiding behind the counter with his shotgun. Jim destined to spend his days alone. Every hoof fall of his horse a kind of earthquake felt a hundred miles away, warning everyone. Maker of ghost towns.

He passes his old office yet again, starting to feel like he's stalking his previous self. Main Street, from one end of town to another, back and forth, paved over now but otherwise the same as anything from Louis L'Amour. He's read every one of them, in most cases more than once.

He drives like a good citizen, passes the old green pier that holds nearly all his lake memories, and turns into the driveway, mounts the steps, reenters the sacred ground he's been banished from. No laws hold for long.

His mother in her usual position at the sink. As if the small house is a fort, his father looking out the front window and mother checking the flank, making sure the neighbors don't invade over the fence, trampling the pansies.

"I need to call her," he announces. "I tried to find her but she's hidden away somewhere."

"Jim," his mother says.

"Yeah."

"We can help you. You don't need her."

"It's been a lot of help so far. Real progress. But maybe I'll just call her."

His father hasn't even turned to look. Back of his head, wearing his cap right now, as if he's outside. Big red ears.

Jim steps into the thin hallway. Two small bedrooms separated by a long narrow bathroom with pink carpet. The old electric heater from his earliest memories, the clothes hamper where he was sitting when he first came and saw semen, so surprised and the most amazing relief. The bathroom seemed bigger then, and a kind of sacred ground for being the only place private, his bedroom shared with his older sister and then Gary.

He stands at the toilet and pisses and can smell piss in the carpet. Why carpet a bathroom? Pouches of potpourri on the back of the toilet, crushed roses and cloves and whatever else to battle the piss. The small window high up always open, view of the garage and its bedroom above where each of them moved when they were old enough, though Gary was the first to use it successfully for sex. Privacy wasted on Ginny and Jim, both social misfits with too much time spent working and at church and doing homework. How many did Gary get to have up there?

He flushes and then stands in front of the bathtub, which has been built into its own alcove wallpapered in roses red and pink, so claustrophobic. Even the tub itself is pink. This small space and so many hours, hundreds of hours through the years, the only place to cry after heartbreak, only place to view contraband, only place to think uninterrupted.

He stands at the window and can see the trellis and strange seedpods, like snap peas except grown overlarge, curved and long and sharp like scimitars, brown and so rough and inedible, hell's version of snap peas, what the garden can become. And what did they ever use the backyard for, or the shade from that trellis? He had to mow that small lawn hundreds of times, but no one ever sat there, too boxed in and limited. The places we live so strange, what they might say or fail to say about us.

But this bathroom performing its function even now. No one intruding, no one calling for him. He's allowed as much time here as he wants, and the others will steadfastly ignore that passing, too uncomfortable to contemplate. If he could bring in a sleeping bag and just live right here, he might get through two nights with his parents.

But he steps outside into the hallway and time begins again and momentum and the fight with his family that must have begun before memory. He hasn't even touched the receiver on the phone before he's warned again.

"Just leave her, Jim," Gary says. "Don't look back."

Jim dials the number he knows easily, and she answers right away, her voice more familiar than anything else here. "It's me," he says.

"You're freaking out my family."

"Sorry."

"Donna thinks you're going to kill me. Are you going to kill me before you kill yourself?"

"No."

"And how do I trust this?"

"Can we have our usual talk?"

"There's no such thing. And especially now that you're here."

"Yeah."

"Your parents are hearing this, and Gary?"

"Yeah."

"And you think there can be anything usual?"

"No. You're right."

"They still think I'm the problem?"

"Yeah."

"Well how are you feeling today? Are you okay?"

"No. Not really."

"What are you feeling?"

"Um. Hard to say standing here. I can't think."

"You'll have to just ignore them. I'm not going to see you in person."

"Yeah," Jim says. He's looking at the carpet, thick shag brown with strands of blonde. Almost like a woman's hair, standing on some giant woman's head. Unnoticed up here, inconsequential. Flung out in the next wash.

"I feel shafted," he says. "Thrown away."

"You think I threw you away?"

"Yes."

"I'm trying here, Jim. I'm trying to help you, because I realize everyone else you know is worthless for this. But I need you to be fair."

"Feelings aren't fair."

"I know that."

"Okay. And yeah, I see how it was my fault, cheating on you."

"Twice. Or two sets of times. Who knows how many women each time."

"Yeah."

"Don't do this," Gary says. "Don't torture yourself." He has a hand on Jim's back and is trying to grab the phone with the other.

"Stop. I need to talk with her."

"Can't you see she doesn't help you? She only makes everything worse. All your problems are from her. I'm begging you at this point. You're my brother. Please stop."

Jim is fighting to keep the receiver at his ear as Gary tugs on it.

"You don't have to talk with me if you don't want," Rhoda says. "You can follow your family. It's fine with me."

"No. I need to talk with you. And I need to see you. You have to see me."

Gary has stopped tugging at the phone. Just standing behind Jim now, and Jim doesn't know what he'll do next. This dining room so fucking small, the ceiling about two inches over their heads, everything closing in.

"I need to see you," Jim says again.

"Let's focus on you, Jim. Take a deep breath and let it out slowly and close your eyes. Do it now."

Jim follows what she says, feels the shake and rattle on the exhale and realizes he's panicking.

"Now another deep breath and exhale and just focus inside, in your chest, in your lungs. Just put your attention there. Focus on your breathing. Are you tired?"

"Yes. So tired."

"Just breathe and rest."

"Okay."

"And let's come up with some things you can do today to relax. After we finish our phone call, you can do push-ups and sit-ups and maybe go for a run?"

"Yes."

"That will help you relax and help calm your thoughts. And then you can take a shower."

"Yes."

"Okay. So you have a plan. And when you finish your shower you can call me again, okay?"

"Yes. Thank you." Jim is holding the receiver against his cheek as if it could be her hand. His eyes closed and swaying and focusing on his breath and feeling calmer, feeling a bit better.

"I can't believe you're ten years younger," he says.

"It's all right," she says. "Just focus on your breath and do your push-ups and sit-ups and go for your run, have a nice hot shower, and then we'll talk again. I'll be here for you."

"You're too good."

"I'm not, as you know. But who I am doesn't matter now. You have a plan, and call me after your shower."

"You could talk to me. Maybe vary a bit from the fucking plan."

"I'm trying to help you, Jim."

"Yeah, sorry. Okay. I'll go do my homework."

He hangs up the phone, gets down into push-up position, and begins the routine, safe again? He doesn't feel safe. He feels murderous, so angry suddenly, so he pushes and doesn't stop, goes past his usual thirty-five to forty and fifty, his chest and arms gone vacant, trembling, hollowed out for any strength at all, but he's working from something more than muscle and pushes on to sixty before he collapses.

"How many was that?" Gary asks.

Jim can't breathe, his throat and chest burning. He feels hinged, like his arms are wings, connected too awkwardly to the plates in his upper back. "Sixty," he manages.

"Do you usually do that?"

"What do you think?"

"She makes you self-destructive, even when she says she's helping you."

"Not a time to talk. I have my homework now. Pretend I'm not here."

"We're your family."

"We've already been through this, haven't we?"

Jim starts his sit-ups, hands laced behind his head, swinging all the way forward between his knees and back down again, the knuckles of his spine in the way, hitting too hard even on carpet. His body not made well for anything, half-suited to any purpose.

He does a hundred, compacting his gut into a knot, then lies back and smells dust. "Mostly skin I'm breathing now," he says. "Sloughed-off skin from all the years. Yours and mine and Ginny's and Mom's and Dad's. I wonder what years I'm breathing right now. Can I breathe from when we were kids?"

A slight buzz in his nose from dust, an allergen. He can feel the caverns in his forehead, the frontal sinuses, puckering, that strange metallic tug, metallic perhaps from blood, from iron. He's had sinus problems for so long.

The dust floating thick above the carpet throughout the entire house, up to perhaps knee level in high concentration and thinning above that, an atmosphere in different bands. The nostalgiasphere first, the layer most dense, where he's lying now, a region of immense weight where time can slow or even stop moving and echoes of sound and smell and feeling can travel forever. Catfish with their wide tendriled mouths patrolling here as leviathans, fallen birds and smell of gun smoke and blood and everything grown larger. A place intent on suffocation, place of Bible stories with children ripped in half, towers falling, tongues without words, locusts descending. The sea parted and held back by a single human hand and the weight of that ready to rush in again, mountains of water overhanging and bending light and even the water smells of blood and can transform, all mutable here, nothing remaining separate or safe.

Above that the beginning of loss of memory and self, the first thinning, burial without earth, dissipation only, disconnection from all that was felt or known before, and so it can't have any name. Its nature is to remove name and then everything behind the name, until we reach the band above, where we normally live and breathe our adult lives, wondering whether something has been forgotten. All decision without basis, all feeling a remnant only. A thousand names and none of them matter. The confusosphere or fuckosphere, all you get to know from now on, only known antidote death.

"You wouldn't believe how much your religion has fucked my head, Mom," Jim says. "I just thought of plagues and the parting of the Red Sea and that baby ripped in half, and even now as I speak I'm thinking of new ones, of the reed basket floating and snakes and Abraham's knife raised and who knows what else. What a fucking nightmare you gave me." David's stone buzzing through the air and Goliath's forehead wait- ing. How hot it must have been then in the endless desert, always desert. Sand closing in on everyone, flooding from all sides, the walls of the ark crushed, not meant for this kind of ocean, all the animals two by two filling their mouths with it as they try to breathe.

He has to get outside. Strange to run in jeans and boots and a flannel shirt, but that's what he's wearing. "I'm going for a run," he says, and he's out that creaky metal door again. At least it's not hot. A breeze just coming up, dark ripples on the water.

The problem is two by two. That has always been the prob- lem. If it weren't for sex and everything attached to it, his life would have been fine. He's always worked hard, he didn't commit crimes, he was smart, and all would have been easy if not for sex. Or even if the desire for sex had been two by two, the desire for only one woman. He would have been fine in that case also. But desire is never for one. There's always another, and always disgust and shame and guilt to go along with the relentless need.

Heavy clomp of his boots on pavement. He's going to destroy his ankles. He's run plenty of times in the forest and across glades, firing off shots at a deer or chasing after one he's wounded. Pavement, though, and the impact.

From the very beginning, even from junior high, he had a sense of doom about picking one and about whether he would be picked. Every human rule, everything that holds us together, based on the lie of two by two, the basis for all law and social organization, and so everything destined to be broken. If he could destroy it all, every church and court and group with any authority, from the PTA to the Senate, he would. Every last bit of it burned to the ground because it was based on something impossible and untrue.

"Fuck!" he yells, and punches himself in the head. But that hurts more than he would have imagined, so he won't do that again. He keeps running past the elementary school, inland, away from the lake, feeling the throb of his head and tightness in his lungs and legs. His body still working. He stays in shape only so he can fuck. Otherwise he would sit in the dark and eat ice cream all day.

He doesn't even like Rhoda. Her condescension though she's younger. The thinness of her lips when she kisses him. Or what she knows about him, everything she knows. He's never been able to hide anything from her. But he has this desperation for her, wants her right now. Disgust and self-hate and as much need as a child. He's had her, and it wasn't enough. So how can he still want her? How can we be so imbecilic? What is it inside us that just endlessly misunderstands everything?

He can feel the sockets of his knees, the balls grinding, and his ankles are made of pins that could shatter. He stops and bends over, panting, dizzy, sits down in the road. "Just run me over," he says. "God that would be so much simpler."

The problem is that his existence continues. He doesn't just utter that and then vanish or cut ahead to another time when something else might happen. He's still sitting in the middle of the road, still has to wait through every moment, never able to fast-forward.

He lies down, because maybe a car will be less likely to see him then. This pavement connects to the highway, and because of that connects to pavement everywhere else in the lower forty-eight. He could walk without touching earth all the way to Florida or Maine. Only Alaska is cut off by dirt and gravel road, which is perhaps why he moved there, to escape. But the only difference is four-wheel drive. Still complete worship of the car.

He turns over on his stomach, feeling some warmth from the asphalt, even on an overcast day, then rolls a couple times, tucks his arms, like a worm.

But this is only desperation, trying to find time away from his head, and it's not fooled. Time still ticking too slowly, only a minute or two passed.

So he stands and runs again, waiting for the activity to kick in and kill his thoughts. Every life reduced to the number of footfalls spent trying to run away from that life. How amazing it must have felt to just pull the trigger and blast him in the back and change everything. And then refuse all consequence, refuse to stay for all that would happen afterward, putting the pistol to her head. So fast. She lived as a murderer for maybe a couple minutes, but because no one knew, she never lived as a murderer at all. We only are something when someone else knows, and it can't be one person. It has to be the group. That's when we become. What she did was no different than dreaming until the group knew.

He wishes he had noticed her more and could remember her more. Plenty of time spent together but he was only half watching, as we are most of the time. He wonders about signs, and responsibility. Was her family supposed to save her?

Is his family supposed to save him? That's the entire purpose of this trip, to come down and visit the family and be saved. And Gary is trying at least, not that it matters.

She was mean. There's no doubt about that. Even her little dog was mean. Prune. What a name for a dog.

What matters now is that Jim has to figure out how to become only a suicide and not a mass murderer. That's the high goal he can reach for, the fruit of a life of hard work. Congratulations. When he was rolling on the asphalt, the magnum at his back felt gargantuan and certainly unyielding. And so heavy now while running. It will have its day.

The sky is puckering, aiming at him, and shits out a light drizzle to accompany his run. Nothing romantic, no storm to help him discover something, just enough to annoy.

But the run is doing its work. A natural painkiller for body and soul, some easing further in as his lungs and legs struggle. He has to keep pushing, and that focus is perhaps what does it. He makes an enormous square and comes back in along the waterfront and is watching the green pier in its jagged lurching until it calls him to climb its barricade, a fan of metal spikes around each side to keep intruders away. Jim can't be kept away, though. He has no fear at this point, doesn't care if he falls, clings to spike and wire and is standing on wood planking soon enough. Long thin walkway of his childhood over the tules and water, with a roofed area at the end and a picnic table also green and a slanting walkway down to the float where he swam and fished a million times, its four piles chewed away to half their strength over all these years despite the softened touch of rollers. At this point the entire pier needs to be replaced.

But he doesn't walk down, not yet. Stands on the upper deck at the railing looking out to a couple miles of open water and the hills on the far side. The lake so big, distance fading from the rain, hills disappeared as he watches, erased, and the water shortened, no droplets visible on the surface but only a general darkening, all pewter gone, every gray surface turning black as if water could be charred, invisible flame and from what source? From above or below? So much of what we see must be formed by heat but never seen. A burning world unnoticed.

Jim climbs the railing and stands crouched on top, his head bent against the roof above. How far down the water seemed when he was a kid, a forever fall. He jumps now as he did then, flinging himself out and away from all safety, but the fall is so brief, only the first hint of suspension, and then he plunges, carried low by the weight of his boots and jeans. Colder than he remembered, thinking of summers and forgetting this is winter still. Shock of it everywhere, his breath gone, and getting colder still, kicking and pulling hard with his arms to fight upward. Cold water thinner. He's falling through it so easily, away from air and light. Interesting to feel himself struggle to live, as if his life is a precious thing, to take that next breath. His body forgotten that this is no longer urgent.

Jim surfaces and breathes, automatic, without debate, but then he relaxes and lets himself fall again and exhales slowly, steadily, letting all air go and his body sink, trying to stay relaxed despite the cold. Feeling of pressure in his ears, and of course he can't equalize with his bad sinuses, and the pain is so pointed he kicks upward again and forgets and surfaces again. What he might be or want hidden so deeply in all that simply carries on.

He swims toward the float without deciding, just does it, watching, and then climbs the aluminum bars of a new swim ladder, not at all the same as the ladders of years past in steel and wood meant to decay.

Jim stands in his thick clothing so heavy and suddenly remembers the pistol, terrified he's lost it, but when he reaches back quick it's still there, somehow, intent on its purpose, refusing to be dismissed, lodged in him for better or worse and impervious to elements. He could fire it underwater, even. It would still work, the powder encased in that shell, the sealed firing pin. Jim the Navy Seal, come to free the tules from the carp.

He drips for a while, stands there a wet ghost unnoticed until the shivering sets in more and gets his teeth chattering, which strikes him as funny. He shifts his jaw from side to side to get different chatters, adds a low moan to become a stuttering ghost, raises his arms to scare the children. Dances a bit on the float, which pitches and bobs under his weight, the way all ground should, responsive. The entire world should lurch in response to us.

The poles at the corners are limiting his effect, though, rollers able to shift only a few inches to any side. He wants a float unpinned, free, wants to stand on a corner and raise a mountain with his weight. So he pitches off the edge into the tules and stink water, all the rot, surprised to sink over his head again, struggling and pulling at the long reeds which are rough on his hands, little knives if grabbed too fast. A surface of yellow scum and froth and fish bloat. His boots find slippery mud and soft earth that he sinks through to his shins but he rises nonetheless, unstoppable, until there's sand under his boots and he towers again as tall as the tules and then taller still, walking up onto the chunks of cement slippery with green algae that looks like hair, walking again on scalp and remaining untouched, not brought down. So nimble, so careful not to come to any harm.

He rises to the fence and stands holding links in his fingers as a car passes and the passenger stares at him. Some lake beast recognized finally but too late, the town without enough warning to set up searchlights and barricades and land mines. "I'm here," Jim says. "I'm already here."

He climbs the fence and is really starting to resent it, the way he gets stabbed at the top and can't get any purchase with his boots. But soon enough he's on the other side, facing all the waterfront association homes tucked away behind their hedges. A long rectangle for each, shape of a life, corners marked. What if none of this had happened? What if all of life had been imagined differently? He might have had a chance. This version does not work for him.

Time. The entire ball of wax. He sits playing pinochle, freshly showered and warmed and wearing more of Gary's clothing, baggy flannel shirt. Partnered with his mother, who is debating a bid of twenty-nine.

"Jesus, Mom," he says. "Just do it. Your whole life going too low on the bids, missing so many lead hands, and all for what? What was going to happen?"

No one is responding to him. A secret pact they've all made while he was away.

She looks so worried, afraid of the twelve cards fanned out in her hand, but the cards must be good. She never bids at all unless it's the kind of hand that would cause no hesitation in anyone else. Sighing, actually sighing and shaking her head, as if terrible things are coming, impossible to avoid.

"I bid once," he says. "That means I have either a lead hand or a helping hand. Either way you're safe to bid again. You must have cards or you wouldn't have bid at all. You never bid a helping hand, so usually I'm having to take the lead with no information. Whereas here all knowledge has been laid at your feet. And it's only twenty-nine. No need for thought at all until you hit thirty-five."

Still staring at her cards, mouth tight and worried, head shaking back and forth in recognition of certain doom.

"Seriously, what's the worst that can happen?" he asks.

"Well I guess I'll say twenty-nine," she says in the most defeated voice, as if the wagon train has just been burned and she's contemplating the far mountains, calculating the hundreds of miles of unknown territory still to cross.

"Thirty," Gary says.

"Sure you don't want to evaluate the risk first?" Jim asks. Gary with a sour face.

"And I shall pass, Mom, but in full support of your lead hand, as expressed already through my initial bid. All anxiety and uncertainty burned away in an instant."

His dad folds his cards and drops them on the table, a silent pass developed years ago to match his personal flair. He rubs at one of his ears, other arm folded over whatever chest exists above that great mound of gut.

Back to his mother now, who looks even more worried.

"All pretty simple," Jim says. "It's the two of you bidding for the lead, and you can't let him have it for thirty, so of course you're going to say thirty-one now. Thirty-three will also be automatic. Thought doesn't have to begin until thirty-five."

"Thirty-one," she says, but not as a bid, only as a contemplation, the enormity of it, whether it can be reached.

"I wonder if this is what got me," Jim says. "This worry. Maybe this is the base on which all the rest has been built."

"Just play the game," Gary says. "No need for the comments. We've been playing since we were kids. Mom's been playing even longer."

"But she's frozen with fear. Look at this. Frozen at the prospect of making a low bid with a good hand and a partner who has help. Doesn't any of that strike you as strange?"

"Just let her decide. It's her hand."

"But it's not. This is a partner game. What she does or doesn't do is my score also."

"Well be a good partner then and shut up."

His mother still searching the cards as if they hold secret signs, indications of a larger and certainly malevolent universe, trying to avoid wrath and fury but unable to read.

He puts down his cards and lays his arms out on the card table toward her. "The world will not end," he says. "Or at least not for this reason. Please just say thirty-one."

"Oh," she says. "Thirty-one."

"Thirty-two," Gary says.

"Now thirty-three, Mom. Just say thirty-three."

Her mouth open slightly in the terror of it all. "Thirty-three," she ponders again, in the voice they all know is not a bid but only for her own consideration, testing its weight. One hand up to her chest, comforting herself. The unhappiness on her face, unguarded. This is when she can be seen, the most unselfconscious moment he might witness.

"I guess I'll have to pass," she says.

"No," he says.

"Diamonds," Gary says, and his father picks up his hand, awaking from slumber to sort through what four cards to send.

"I was going in clubs," his mother says to him, her eyes liquid. The beginning of the table talk. They always ask to find out what would have been. It drives more serious pinochle players crazy.

"No," he says. "I'm not telling you what I have. No more of that. If you want to find out, you have to bid."

"Jim," she says.

"No. I'm tired of the second-guessed life and the regret if it turns out we had the double run or a double pinochle. It has poisoned everything. I'm always thinking about what if I had visited Rhoda that time and not worried what the ticket cost, or what if I had never returned Gloria's interest, what if I still had my family, or what if I had let myself drink and relax in high school or decided not to follow Dad into dentistry. All the thousands of fucking pounds of regret I'm carrying around every day. So you don't get to know whether I had any clubs."

"I had eight clubs. I only needed a jack."

"You had eight clubs!"

"Keep your voice down."

"Jesus, Mom." He takes the jack of clubs from his hand and throws it into the middle of the table. "There. Happy? All that didn't happen. Let's cover ourselves in all that might have been. I've been smearing it over my face like shit for years now."

"Jim," Gary says.

"Yeah yeah."

"Pick up your card."

"What's the point? I'm calling Rhoda." Jim rises and leaves his cards faceup on the table, destroying the hand. "All the thousands of hands we've played over the years, what a monumental waste of time. And how pathetic, that we can relate to each other only in this way. Only killing or cards. Occasional waterskiing or bowling. It's all we know."

His mother looking aggrieved, and he hates hurting her. "Jesus, Mom," he says. "Always hurt, but that's the way you made it. Apparently you like it."

Her mouth open as if she might say something, but of course she doesn't, and he feels so guilty he has to turn away, lurches for the phone, a lifeline. Rhoda had better be there right now.

He turns the dial for each of her numbers, the most important code in his life, and luckily she answers. "I'm losing it," he says. "Mom just passed at thirty-two with eight clubs in her hand. And terrified. As if the cards might come alive and kill us all."

"It's okay, Jim," she says. "Your family will always have their problems, but you don't have to fix them."

"Hm," he says. "I guess that does help. I don't have to fix them."

"Yeah, you don't. You don't have to do anything about them, nothing at all, no pressure. You don't even have to visit them. You're free to leave right now. Always free, not locked in. Remember that."

"Okay. I want to see you."

"No."

"Why not?"

"We've been through this."

"You see me right now. And I mean right fucking now. I need more than just a chat on the phone. And when you think about all our years together, you'd think you could give me that. Just half an hour or something in person. Is it really too much to ask?"

No response from Rhoda, which gives him hope. She's thinking. He can hear his breathing, and he holds back from saying anything more. He knows that even one more word

will spoil it. Gary drifts toward him and Jim holds out a palm
telling him to back off. Gary had better not fuck this up now.

"Okay, Jim," she says finally. "This once. I don't think it's
a good idea, but I'll meet you and we can talk. But only this
once."

"Thank you."

"No," Gary says. "Don't go. This is not a good idea."

Jim turns away toward the wall. "Where?" he asks.

"At the diner."

"I don't want to see Donna. We'll never be able to talk with
her there. She won't even let me inside probably."

"I guess you're right."

"The little motel where we used to meet. Private. No
one to overhear. I want to be able to talk freely. I don't want
some idiots listening in."

"That's not a good idea, being alone together in a motel
room."

"I need to be able to talk. Please."

A long pause and he thinks he's asked too much, pushed
too far.

"Okay," she says.

Doom. Hard to know whether it exists, but then sometimes you can feel it happening. When too much weight has congregated.

The motel is not in the center of town but out along the lakefront, discreet. He looks at the water as he drives, going slowly, not wanting to attract attention. Coots all along the edge, thin black necks pumping as they swim, always fleeing, the equivalent of rats. Everyone shoots them out of boredom and still their numbers are relentless. White bill making an easy target.

He wonders what she'll be wearing. Hoping for lingerie beneath. Most likely jeans and a sweater. Most likely not made up. And has she just come from Rich?

She'll treat him like a child, even though he's older, smarter, has worked harder, knows more. But he has to go along with that, because she holds the keys to the kingdom.

"What am I doing," he says aloud. "What are you doing, Jim? What is today?"

What else is there left to do? He hasn't seen his friends. John Lampson, only a short drive from here, in Kelseyville, and Tom Kalfsbeck in Williams. Maybe one of them is the key. Maybe he'll meet John for a game of chess and find something new, a sudden rush of feeling as they both bend over the board and he'll realize he was gay all along and that was the cause of despair, and after they get together Jim will

158

feel mental illness dissipate, find out it never existed. That's the story he wants, something uplifting that reaffirms he was always good, something to make him innocent.

But friends don't make us. They don't have the power of family. And sex is despair and for Jim it is with women and particularly this woman, and things will never work out with her.

Facts. Important to stick with the facts. The lake doesn't care, or the patches of tules or ducks or coots, or the gray sky above, or any of the people here. Facts are always lonely.

He pulls into the gravel lot. Only eight or ten rooms, ranch style from when he was a kid, painted light blue now but so many colors over the years. Small windows looking over the road to the lakefront houses and water beyond. One possible place, as good as any.

He walks to reception, doesn't recognize the woman behind the counter. He's been away so long. He used to know everyone in this town.

He pays in cash, just to slow the police down a bit. They won't know at first who they're looking for.

He walks the wooden deck along the rooms, old wood, a sidewalk from the Wild West, enjoying the heavy clomp of his boots, wishing he had spurs. At the end of every western some showdown, and what he loves most is the quiet then. The only real peace. Struggle all the way along, but right before the final gunfight all is calm and there's room to breathe and everyone can be their best selves. They can love their families and be good to their friends, can be ready to die nobly, and can say pithy things. There's a bit of humor finally. But he's missing the rest of the cast. No one to have those touching final conversations with, no chance to make some thematic observation, something about how if it would ever just rain we could be clean, or this prairie was never meant for things to grow.

What he likes is the simplicity. Six-shooters and nothing to stop them, only leather and wood, nowhere safe, and the law no more than a badge, not SWAT teams in riot gear. Fate decided by individuals without waiting for a government larger than god. Now there's no getting away, no riding a horse hard into the desert. Now there's only a short time and chips all in. Once it starts it ends quickly.

The room is small and dimly lit, no overhead but only the two bedside lamps. Narrow double bed, the mattress thin. He wonders if they've been in this room before. Too long ago and back then he didn't care which room. No dresser or desk. One small chair by the window, made for waiting, and so he sits there, curtains open, overcast light. Feels so sad, so relentlessly sad and lost, but he tries to experience it, last moments and the quiet and the easy sense, a new sense, that it won't have to be endured forever. A calming.

This makes him worse, that it feels easier in the end. Unfair. After all he's suffered, all the nights of insomnia and terrible pain and despair when he fought so hard to keep from pulling the trigger. And then to pull the trigger when he doesn't feel that bad, but apparently that's often when it happens. On a small upswing, when the suicide feels a bit better and has the energy finally to do it. He knows too much now about the patterns and statistics of suicide, watching himself and making commentary along the way. Another insult.

His mother's Christianity never gone. Still this desire to be good even as he knows what he's going to do. The main failure of his life, his inability to grab hold of that weed and yank it out. Wrapped around everything inside and in him so long it has become indistinguishable from flesh and feeling and thought, all that might be called him. Nothing can be separated out as his own.

The stranger who comes to town might as well be Jesus himself in every western. Never recognized by the townsfolk, always looked at with suspicion, but he's here to deliver justice, defeat evil, and offer redemption. In his actions a model of goodness, because he has what no human can ever have, a solid core. The stranger in a western never changes, never can be broken, knows right and wrong absolutely and from the beginning and was born into the world this way and will leave untouched. This could never be Jim. He can carry the six-shooter and wear the spurs but inside he has no idea what to do and anything can change him at any moment and he can only read signs of himself later and wonder who he was, never know who he is.

Goodness, the most dangerous idea. That he should have been good, that's what will make him pull the trigger.

He wonders if she's not coming. Too long a delay. He can't bear the drifting. He needs her to come now. He stands because maybe that will help. "You'd better fucking come," he says. "You owe me that."

The floor is wood, actual wood planks. Not some nasty carpet or plywood or concrete. He's grateful for this at least. Uneven and painted dark blue but the real thing. Far too depressing if the end were on carpet.

"It will be real pretty," he says, and he likes the sound of his voice, a bit of a twang. "Real pretty." Her blood sprayed on the walls and his on the ceiling. Bits of bone and flesh. The blood running the planks and seeping down through gaps, darkening with time. The magnum so loud, though, it won't be much time. That door will be open again in minutes.

He stood in her parents' living room so many times, such a large space, carpeted, multilevel with glass sliders leading out to the pool. He imagines the glass was blasted by stray pellets. She would have been coming from the hallway, such a long and wide hallway it was kind of crazy, leading to four bedrooms and the large office that held a hundred guns in glass cases. The hallways dimly lit and the gun room with so many small lights to showcase antique pistols and hex-barreled rifles. Classic shotguns with the most beautiful carvings in their wooden stocks and even etched designs along the steel barrels. Each worth thousands, a few perhaps even more than that. A fortune in that room. Red velvet lining the glass cases, plush. And mostly a sense of weight. All guns so heavy before, the castings so thick. His .44 magnum about the heaviest pistol you can buy now, but slim and light by comparison to the dragoons. He thinks that's what they were called. Fancy French names for some of the guns. Like old ships, so many names we no longer use.

He wants to know which pistol she picked, and why. Rhoda has never told him. Picked carefully or without any thought at all? No one will ever know that. And what about the shotgun? Something beautiful? One particularly meaningful to him? She must have had to listen to him talk endlessly about each of those guns. You don't put together that kind of collection without obsession.

Rhoda's old Datsun B210, dark green, pulls onto the gravel near the office. She'll be asking which room. Wearing a yellow sweater and jeans, and he remembers that sweater from a photo of the two of them in Oregon, when the boat was being built, standing in front of the apartment complex. He had a beard then and hair getting longer, becoming a fisherman, dreaming of this perfect aluminum boat cutting through Alaskan waves and a life entirely free. Saying fuck you to land and cars and people, an early sign of the euphoria. A dream of escape, not understanding yet that there's never escape while we still breathe.

No sound of her walking. Only tennis shoes, not heels. She should have dressed differently for this. Perhaps didn't understand the importance.

He opens the door for her. "Thank you," he says. "Thank you for coming."

"You don't look too bad," she says, stepping inside. "I thought you'd look worse. But what happened to your face?"

"A few scuffles with Gary and the woods."

She gives him a hug, the shock of it almost too much, the feeling of warmth and her body pressed close to his, the overwhelming fullness. But her hand touches the pistol. "What's this?"

He reaches back to pull it free. Solid in his grip. Loaded. He could just press it now to her neck and shoot down through her and she'd be done, unstrung and collapsed instantly. "I'll put it away." He sets it on the chair by the window. It can keep guard by itself. Anything might happen now. She might take it and shoot him, all reversed.

"You shouldn't have that," she says, and her arms are around him again. He wonders what this means.

"I know. But I'm not willing to leave it with anyone. It's my insurance policy. Sometimes the only way I can get through the night is knowing there's a quick way out. Just having it available. I need that. Having no way out would be unbearable."

"Jim," she says, her head pressed against his chest now. He closes his eyes. She's holding him so tightly and this feels so perfect, he doesn't know how he could have failed to recognize it before.

"This is perfect," he says.

"Jim."

"Really. Just feel this. We can go back. Forget everything. Just feel this now and you know it's true."

She lets go of him then and he regrets saying too much, losing her.

"Sorry," he says, and pulls her to him again, but she pushes away.

"We should talk, Jim. We need to find a way for you to know that it's over and that's okay. Talk about how you move on from here."

"That's not the talk I want."

"I know."

He feels lost standing there separate, so he sits down on the bed and then lies back, closes his eyes.

She sits beside him. "I know you loved me," she says. "But you didn't really love me. And that's why you're going to be okay now. Remember what it felt like when we were married, when you had me completely, all to yourself, and that wasn't what you wanted, not really. Remember the weight of that and how you felt trapped, how the months ahead were things to get through. Remember us on the boat, all those hours day and night, and Gary there, only the three of us, and how small that felt sometimes, how lonely. I know you want to believe in a dream of us, something to reach for when you're feeling so bad, but it will help you more to remember there was nothing there. You will find love again, something that surprises you, but it won't be with me."

"No," he says, but he doesn't know what he's saying no to. That there will be another woman, or that it was lonely with Rhoda, or just the enormity of having to find some way through. He's been fighting for so long he's exhausted. He can't keep going. "I need to be done."

"That never happens. You know that. We're never done, even in the most stable life."

"Lie down with me."

She does that, to his surprise, and even puts an arm over him, which feels so much better. He tries to remember what it felt like on the boat, how it could have been empty or not enough. Narrow bed, barely holding the two of them, just behind the pilothouse. Everything below decks reserved for the fish holds and engine room. Gary's bunk and an extra in that same room, no privacy, so they had to wait until Gary, and the deckhand if they had one, were on watch, and then they locked the door and he remembers the best sex of his life then. Something about being bucked in the waves, the constant movement, and the short, stolen time they had. He remembers her legs, so thin, and wanting her in his mouth, and remembers having to hold the bunk above to not be thrown.

When they slept, also, he felt so close to her. She was always right on top of him then. Like sleepwalkers having to rise every couple hours for the next watch, falling again so quickly, four or five times a day. An odd existence.

"I don't remember that it wasn't enough. On the boat. I don't remember small or lonely."

"You had times at the helm you just wanted to be alone. Didn't want to talk with me."

He tries to remember that, hundreds of hours staring at the high bow pitching through seas, remembers being concentrated and often grim and worrying about the boat, always some fear of hitting a log or the engine breaking down or the longline getting snagged, as it finally did, crumpling the drum and ending their chances, but he doesn't remember not wanting to talk with her.

"Did that really happen?" he asks.

"Yes. It really did."

"I guess I wasn't there. I missed it somehow. It's not in my memories."

She puts a leg over him and scoots closer, her head on his shoulder. He has both arms around her now, and this is all he wants. How could it ever not have been enough?

Shitty little motel room and yet here's where he could be happy. Just freeze this moment and keep it.

Damp smell of her hair, like the smell of a horse. Her forehead with the adult version of acne, just a bumpiness. She's not really beautiful, and he's always known that, but he's drawn to her anyway. Kisses her forehead now and pulls her closer in his arms.

She seems responsive. He kisses lower, straining to reach her cheek, and she tilts her face up and offers her mouth, exactly as he would have hoped. This moment of willingness is what every man wants. Thin lips but he doesn't care, feels only grateful.

Love. As close as he's ever been, so it must be what love is. A tenderness, one hand cradling the back of her head, and he's moaning, and instantly hard. And he can't pull her close enough to his chest. But what if it has never been love at all? What if he has missed something basic? How would he ever know? If he's never loved, he won't know that.

What makes it seem not like love is the fact that he's watching, still thinking about what's happening. He's still aware, also, that he would not give everything for her, no feeling of full sacrifice, no perfect selflessness. He loves her only because he wants. If she doesn't give him sex right now, he will be unhappy, disappointed, angry, and will not feel love at all. And if some more beautiful woman came along, or even just someone available at the right moment, he would not be faithful.

There was a time with her early on, in the first year or two, when other women disappeared and he would not have wanted anyone else. That did happen. And why couldn't that remain? It would have made things so much simpler.

They're pulling at each other. Sex a kind of wrestling match with an imagined urgency, though no clock is running. He has a hand on her ass, and she reaches down for his dick. All the mechanics of it working and happening. He didn't think she would be willing. He feels confused and lost, then he worries that will kill his boner, but her hand is keeping it up anyway, and then her mouth, and he doesn't know why she's doing so much, why she's decided to give to him. None of it makes sense. She's with a new man and wants to marry him.

Jim can feel his dick going soft in her mouth. He's losing it. "Fucking thoughts," he says. "Why can't I get my head to shut up?"

She stops and comes back up to kiss him on the cheek. "I'm sorry, Jim."

"I want it so bad," he says. "I've wanted to be with you. But I can't stop my head. It just always goes."

"It's okay."

Jim has this long exhale, a kind of sigh and shaking, and then he's crying. Eyes turned to soup suddenly and chest heaving, and he feels like he's drowning, has to get up and go to the bathroom to blow his nose and hawk up all the phlegm in his throat. What a fucking mess.

She wraps her arms around him from behind, pressed all along his back, and he closes his eyes and stands there like that, arms hanging and held by her, and everything feels impossible. Sobbing out of control now, and no idea why, or which reason. Pick one of the dozen. Who cares.

"I'm not going to make it," he says, and that makes him cry harder, the self-pity, and when he tries to hold it back he makes some kind of sound too high-pitched, embarrassing. "Squealing like a fucking pig," he says.

"No, Jim," she says. "You're okay. I'm here now, and you're going to be okay."

"Here now but not tomorrow. With Rich tomorrow."

"Shh."

To be held by her again, after so long. Her thin arms around him, and all the rest blocked from view. Only his own body to look at in the mirror, the way he finishes this life, splotchy red but generally so white from Alaska, no sun, no regular exercise, slumped at the middle and his chest dripping into boobs and his arms too thin. Hair receding and Adam's apple sticking out and lines around his eyes, almost forty but looking like fifty. Despair and depression aging more quickly. He always looked young for his age but not now. An old man at thirty-nine.

His dick small and thin and sad, refusing, receding also. Lost in light brown hair. Curly everywhere, all over his body, so much hair on his forearms and chest, everything about his body so disgusting. He shouldn't have to look at it. No one should ever have to. And to be fair, she wouldn't look good in this mirror either. Harsh florescent light. Difficult to believe we can ever feel desire. Blindest impulse possible.

What's strange is that he's still crying but he's also thinking and watching at the same time and feeling nothing. Someone else's body crying, far away. There are two Jims, and the one not crying, the one feeling nothing, is the one to watch out for, but there's no way to reach him. He's never there. He just controls everything and makes everything seem fake.

He doesn't want her to leave, but she does. He stands naked at the window and watches her go, the pistol beside him unused. He was so certain he would use it.

Shooting her in the left tit while she knelt on the bed. Something like that. And then either putting the barrel to his own head or walking quickly to the pickup to go home to his family, to take them with him, and maybe not only Gary and his parents but maybe also Elizabeth and the kids. That was the decision he was facing. But now there is no beginning. He's left by himself and will never see her again. An end and no beginning.

And he didn't fuck her either. Limp-dick Jim, his new name in this western. Come to town to change nothing and fuck no one and never fire a shot.

He picks up the pistol, feels the cold weight, then tosses it on the bed, where it bounces and lands again. A bit of comedy, the bouncing gun. Here to play.

The heater's not on, and he's naked, so he gets under the covers to warm up. The possibility of shooting her on this bed still exists. Something in him can't catch up to the fact that the opportunity has already passed. This is true generally of his mind. It has lagged, and this is the clearest sign that he doesn't believe the world is real. According to his mind, what happens is only one version.

He still has this feeling that if he could say no in the right way the world would stop. Birds stuck in the sky, water no longer falling. Some refusal of our utter lack of control over our lives.

He would walk out naked and be the only movement. He would climb into the air if he felt like it, step by step, or sit on the lake or sink into solid ground. He would reshape mountains with one finger and knock stars out of the sky at night just by breathing. He would refuse to go back to Fairbanks and his small round brown folding card table. Because that is where he's headed now. If there's no shooting of Rhoda, and because of that no shooting of anyone else, then he's going back to Alaska and there's only one place to sit. Didn't get around to shopping for more furniture, and look at the effect that will have now.

He smiles at the thought of it. Such a stupid joke, his life. So exhausted. Rough feel of the cheap sheets, mildew smell of the old motel, pillow too firm, but somehow he sleeps, mercifully, wakes and it is dark outside. The disorientation of any afternoon nap, waking into an end, the feeling of having lost something. But calmer now with the rest, not feeling as desperate.

He has a boner and has to pee. Tries jacking off, but he can't think of anything in particular and doesn't have any porn and gives up. He wonders whether he will have sex again before he dies. Most likely not. Taken out of the game.

He flicks on the overhead light, which is harsh. Pees and then still feels so groggy from the nap he lies down and falls asleep. Wakes cold, not under the covers, and goes for a hot shower, which is not hot and has almost no pressure, towels off with something about as soft as razor wire, and lies down again.

"Time to go," he says, but he feels comatose and cannot motivate, so he sleeps yet again, and now it must be well and truly the middle of the night. There's no clock in here, but he grabs his watch from his bag and sees almost 1:00 a.m. "Nice one," he says. He won't be able to sleep now. He'll be awake all through the night, and what will he do?

He's starving, so he pulls on Gary's oversized shirt and jeans, like a child playing grown-up. Gary's boots too big also. He steps outside and wishes he had a jacket. Cold now. No one around, no lights on except at the motel office, where he drops his room key in the slot.

The pickup starts reluctantly, shivers to life, and Jim pulls onto the road its only traveler. Slow curves along the lake, the water black, a deeper black than the sky. Patches of tules grown larger in headlights, straining upward and falling to the side, dull green. A car passes, going the other way, leaving town so late. Must be some story there. No one's awake at night in a small place without a story.

Throaty sound of the pickup at low revs, just easing along. Houses along the water all single story and old. More chain-link fences, new. Catalog of a place he should know well, but it comes together into nothing. Only the lake itself might be something.

He wonders whether the diner might be open. Wouldn't be Donna or Jim on the night shift. Must be a McDonald's, also, somewhere in town. In the past it was A&W they always went to, the drive-in, but that wasn't twenty-four hours.

Nothing was open in the middle of the night, not even a gas station. If you didn't sleep at the same time as everyone else you were out of luck.

The darkness is impressive. Moon setting early these days, no stars, overcast black night and the lake refusing to reflect anything, only absorbing what little light there is from thinly spaced street lamps. Dead zones between the lamps, places you could stand invisible. And so little from any houses, only an occasional porch light, and no businesses along here.

He rolls down his window to listen, but it's only his tires and a different tone from the engine. The tires a particularly lonely sound, and he wonders why that is. How does our mind make things like that happen?

What if he could start his mind over right now, just re-enter the world and forget he has any problems and just have a normal night and day? Why is that so hard? Everyone else seems fine.

He can feel the wetness of the air, cooled by the lake. Holds his arm out the window with his hand cupped to catch it. Drives on the wrong side of the road to be closer to the water. Closes his eyes in the straight sections to feel what the movement is like, to be transported.

But he's so hungry that's all he can really think of. He wants a chocolate shake. And a big burger with barbeque sauce and bacon. Our last comfort, food. When nothing else is available. Rhoda gone.

He slows to a crawl at his parents' house. All lights off. All sleeping soundly it seems, without a worry about Jim. The oak in the front yard seems enormous right now, dwarfing the house. The hedge too short, barrier to nothing.

He continues on, slows again near Safeway and his old office, his other zone. A few stray cars forgotten and left in the parking lot. More lights and a private security car, someone staying awake to guard groceries. That has to feel worthless, a fake uniform and no gun, and no one interested in what you're guarding. At least at the cash register he was doing something.

Jim tries to appear menacing, idling the pickup and staring, but at a couple hundred yards staring of course doesn't mean anything. Jim could be a tourist lost on his way to Konocti or Lucerne or some other fascinating local destination.

So Jim moves on, stomach grumbling, thinking of going back and stealing the guy's sandwich. He has no gun, so Jim could just beat him down and take the sandwich and even wear the guy's hat and official shirt.

Nothing is open. He'll have to come to terms with starvation. He passes the diner, which is out cold. A&W also dark. Gas stations closed. The entire center of town a void, not even a bar open.

But as he gets to the new section, toward the highway, there are a few lights and other cars, late-night wanderers, and the golden arches do in fact appear. Disgusting compared even to crap places like A&W or Fosters Freeze, and the enormous delicious bacon burger he imagines cannot exist here, but at least he will not starve. In Alaska the most improbable burgers, just to keep up with the idea of the place. As wide as a plate. No clue where they find the buns. And always offering some exotic meat: Caribou! Moose! Lynx! Lynx not really likely, of course, but who is ever going to check?

He pulls up beside several other pickups to join men with tattoos and baseball caps, which would seem to make them belong, because Lakeport has become such a shitty place, but Jim is the one who belongs here, grew up here. He is the native son, born on these shores.

"Mornin'," he says to the person offering to take his order. A throwback to show who he is. The magnum tucked under his shirt again. He'd like an excuse to use it, so he's not quiet. Speaks in a full voice. Let one of the tattooed fucks notice.

But of course they don't. He orders two fish filet sandwiches, as if they're really going to use a filet for each one instead of mashed up baitfish rammed into a square and deep-fried. Looking forward to the small spooge of tartar sauce and the square of American cheese left on top like a thing forgotten.

He stands at the counter waiting. Only three employees, all wearing hairnets as if they belong in a gang, all fat and soft and greasy, shaped by the food here. The empty heating tray, each sandwich actually made to order this late at night. He should personalize in some way, think of something to ask for, but his mind's a blank.

"Order fifty-one," the woman says when she hands him the tray, as if there might be confusion.

"Let me check the receipt," he says. "Just to make sure I'm fifty-one." He holds it up to the light, examines it, sees a fifty-one. Meanwhile she's holding the tray in the air. "Yep," he says. "I see fifty-one. Two Filet-O-Fish sandwiches and a chocolate shake. Is that what you have there?"

"Yes sir," she says, and she doesn't seem upset. Her job is so fucked that this fits in as a normal interaction. Mouth slightly open because of the extra oxygen needed for all that fat. Cheeks glistening.

"May I have a glass of water?" he asks, taking the tray finally.

"Yes sir," she says and dutifully grabs a paper cup. "Ice?"

"No thanks."

She fills the cup from a dispenser with a perfect small stream, water expertly controlled, and hands it to him with "Enjoy your meal sir." All perfectly performed, the way he performed perfectly all those years as a checker. How many years was it? Maybe seven? Wishing everyone a good day no matter how unfair and insulting they were. Handling how many thousands of cans of soup and beans and cartons of milk. A large portion of his life spent that way. More time doing that than just about anything else except dentistry. Sleep has claimed the most hours probably, back when he was able to sleep, but after that standing beside a patient and after that standing beside groceries. Varicose veins now in both calves.

He sits by one of the front windows, lit up for all passers to see, and consoles himself with the chocolate shake, which is more like clay slush with a memory of Hershey's. Feeling of an impending stomachache even with the first mouthful, some pukey foreknowledge built into the taste.

And this is only the beginning of the night. The night will be long.

Jim lies on his back on the floating dock at the end of the green pier. The four pillars rising around him darker shadows in the greater dark, reminders of the apostles.

He has scaled the chain-link fence again and climbed the barrier of spikes and dodged every sand trap and wall of poison darts and swinging grindstone, leapt through fire and over snakes and outrun demons. The apostles not so far removed from that. He has seen photos of their pillars at Ephesus in Turkey, waved in Sunday school to prove these men were real and known, walking among the ancients. Maybe a couple thousand years more, though, to the Egyptians and pyramids. He was never great with dates. All of it pancakes into one dusty ancient day, one day in which the Egyptians rose and fell and also the Greeks and Romans and Chinese and Persians and all the others. Really that's what has happened in his mind. All of that remembered as essentially the same day, the same one point of memory. The ancients can provide myth only, not history.

Even seeing the photos of the pillars he has never believed the apostles were real. Accounts of their voyages along the Turkish coast and sending letters, but impossible to believe. And so boring. I bring good news. The Good News Bible. News, brother, in which nothing happens. Your soul is saved. John arriving on some big beach and telling the kids playing in the sand, hey, your sins are erased. All you have to do is hand over your cash and let him into your heart. A fund-raising trip for the early church. You have no idea our plans. We're going to find new shores, maybe a whole new world, and sell Jesus for gold. We'll build chandeliers hung by golden ropes, all paid for by kids as poor as you, wearing scraps, because there will be a billion of you.

But that's not really his church. His mother Lutheran, and technically he's Lutheran, though he has no idea what it means. In all those hundreds of days in church, not once did they talk about what they were. Not once did they say, here's the Catholic Church and what they believe, and now here's the Lutheran Church and what we believe, and here are the reasons for the differences. And the Old Testament and the New Testament. He knows they're following the new, but what are they supposed to do with the old?

Never any explanation for what he is supposed to believe or for the culture that made him. Only requirements were to sing, stand at the right times, hand over cash, and be polite.

Why it matters is that religion is the closest he can come to some sense of how he was made and who he is now. It's the thing we all agree on without ever knowing what it is. And that must be the cause of the problem, because where else can he look?

The float is rocking him now, small waves come from where? Who is on the lake in the middle of the night? No sound of any boat. The waves were made by something and have to be explained, but nothing we know of fits. Too small and close together to be boat waves. Too sudden and brief to be from wind. Too large and too many to come from a swim-mer. So there must be something larger swimming in the lake, breaking the surface for a moment and then submerging again. Not breaching but quieter than that, just lifting some enormous mass above the surface and then submerging quickly, and that causes a ring of small quick ripples to go in all directions, and Jim happened to be here to register them, perhaps the only one to do so. Otherwise God would not have been known. Jim the only priest, and he will have to walk now back to McDonald's, a pilgrimage. He should lose a shoe along the way to create more struggle, a bit of drama. He'll throw open the glass doors one-shoed and breathless and shout proof finally of God. His ripples felt, his existence. As far as I can tell, he's like a carp but maybe a hundred feet long. Smell of rot, just like in the tules. Living in the deeper sections because these waves were small and smooth and regular so they had traveled far. If we go depth charge the middle of the lake, we might finally see the face of God.

The tattooed masses will follow him out kissing their arms for luck. Talismans everywhere across their skins because they knew this moment was coming, knew all previous pantheons would have to rise up together to defeat the one larger god. Snakes and anchors, Ashleys and Marias and more mysterious gods known only by initials. Hearts and skulls and other body parts that have transcended flesh, brightly colored birds and crosses, swastikas, blood, and even golden-scaled fish, closest gods to this one and most able to form a sacred net. The navy won't get here in time. It will take days for even the most modern cruisers to plow their way through land, Lakeport not close at all to the sea, so this fairy ring of inscribed gods will be the first attack.

Into the water, all of them, swimming in dark night toward God, fearless, wanting to finally touch. No thought of whether they'll have enough strength to return to shore, and so they venture on for half a mile, shedding shoes and jeans and shirts to not be dragged down, and all light is gone this far out, only occasional flashes as water is flung, and still they swim, slower now, a mile out, their numbers slimmer perhaps by a few but no less committed, throwing each arm forward toward knowledge, kicking, impatient for the body to catch up, the body always a weight and barrier and better shed. The last swimmers can no longer raise their arms but only stroke slowly beneath the surface, all quiet, the faithful still buoyed by hope and watching the darkness ahead for any sign, expecting something to surface until they've gone below, limbs locked and breath gone, and even then as they descend they are waiting for the embrace.

Word has spread about God and the faithful who have gone to find it and capture or destroy it. A new crowd gathered at the shore, and someone has thought of all the Fourth of July fireworks and the fireworks barge, so they're hooking up a jet boat to it now, one of the supercharged jobs sounding like a Harley and spitting smoke into the air. Actual sparks coming out its exhausts, raised like fires to heaven. Slick orange paint job and "69" decaled on the side. The plan is to depth charge God with this payload, delivered right now at high speed. The driver is upset he won't be able to display his magnificent rooster tail of water behind the boat, because that would get the fireworks wet, but he's otherwise pleased to have been chosen.

Others want to be the chosen, also, and they're swimming out to the barge and trying to climb aboard, so the whole thing is dangerously low and heaving and the already chosen are kicking others in the head to keep them from boarding. Screams of the faithful in the wakened night, and all of Lakeport brightening, lights along the shore, other boats arriving, the beach awash in crisscrossed wakes.

His mother's church group will be there, in their sixties and seventies, carrying dishes for a potluck. Her famous tuna casserole baked with an entire bag of potato chips to feed the faithful.

One of the local kids is selling bread crumbs to feed the ducks, who must think night has passed and it's now day. A man is offering five minutes on his binoculars for five dollars. Prostitutes are offering one last embrace before the end. A local minister has appeared to explain none of this is true, but he's being ignored.

The jet-boat driver has pulled the towline taut and then suddenly guns it, engine splitting the air, a crackling sound. The fireworks barge lurches forward and the masses on board all shift aft at an angle, hitting like dominoes and going down, the ones at the rear thrown overboard, a great splash and then moans and shouts of lost providence.

The barge creates an enormous wake, and the jet boat's bow is pointed skyward, the driver unable to see where he's going, but he keeps it gunned anyway and the chosen battle for handholds, the losers falling away into the water.

The jet-boat driver guided by faith, view blocked and night too dark anyway, and no signposts to where God might be. Derelict pervert boat owner transformed into high priest, and he clings to the wheel as gravity pulls him backward, keeps the big accelerator plate pinned until he blows the engine, a final shot of fire into the sky and the bow comes down with a slap and the barge glides forward and slows until it bumps his boat gently, companionably.

New leaders now emerging on the barge, fights over what to do with the fireworks: strap them to the bodies of divers to take down as low as possible, or sink the barge after one big fuse is lit, or aim each rocket downward and let it torpedo. The recurring problem in all the discussions is that the fireworks can't get wet. They don't move or explode or work in any way once they hit water. Reaching God very frustrating in this way. Why can't he come to the surface again?

In the end there's nothing to do except light the fireworks from the barge and have a show, Fourth of July early. Brilliant constellations in the sky above, mirrored on the water, and perhaps God will be impressed and want to see. But of course he never surfaces again, and Jim's one contact with him was the only contact, so Jim is burned alive and his bones sawn into pieces afterward to keep a small relic in each house of the faithful. This is the best use of his life he can think of.

The air cold and damp, and no visitation of god and no crowd or carnival gathered. Jim's life still without event. The problem is the struggle against nothing. And the pain in his head.

He can't lie on the float and just feel each curl of pain, so he's up again, without even making the decision, and climbing around the spiky barrier then over the fence. No car passing to see him. He crosses the street to his parents' house, where he's parked the truck in the drive, and continues past to the garage, flicks on the light to see all the antlers, all the bucks they've killed over the years.

Patches of hair still clinging to dried hide. Most looking bleached by time but a few racks still dark with velvet. He's never really understood velvet. Some protective covering when the antler is growing, mossy, but why not regular? Why do only a few have it in the fall?

Each of these sets of antlers was supposed to be a memory, a record, and he was there every year since he was a boy, but they're all so similar he can recognize only a handful. So many guttings, the ripping sound of a knife through hide, impossible to locate each and connect it to the correct antlers, impossible to remember if this was in the lower glades or bear wallow or the burn and who might have been there and who took the shot. Even his own he wouldn't be able to claim now.

The dust in here making his sinus headache worse. The cold too. The bone of the skull so delicate, all the chambers, endless division, paper thin, visible on the underside of every trophy here, but what he doesn't understand is where pain and pressure come from, how they're possible. Each chamber fills with a mucus, and even if it's infected and green and thick, so what? It's still only snot. There's no pump to pressurize. It's not like hydraulics on a boat. It must be that nerves are made too sensitive, lying just over the wafers of bone.

All the mysteries of pain he's seen in dentistry, the patients who are not numbed by the first shot or even the next, the irregular pattern of nerves, unmapped and out of place. It should all be very simple, the one trigeminal nerve on each side of the face, in three branches, to lower jaw, upper jaw, and forehead. But it's not always that simple. One shot to block the mandibular branch and all pain to the lower jaw gone. He can drill away in tooth and bone and only the sound causes terror. But then a patient appears whose pain is not blocked, and Jim is reduced to witch doctor, all science gone and stabbing into the dark.

Ghost pain, also, teeth that hurt long after, weeks after, when there's no reason or even a tooth left at all. Only the desire for pain. What is Jim supposed to do then? The term used for mysteries is "atypical facial pain," which just means who the hell knows. And what is he supposed to do for himself now? Knowing this pain comes from another branch of the same nerve that reaches into his lower jaw is not helpful. Semilunar ganglions the most beautiful half-moons shining just beneath the skin of his temples, the face a divided sphere, but the spaces are so vast. When he closes his eyes, he cannot believe all of this is happening within a few inches. Comets of pain flung in arcs and burning out only to be reborn again, and all from the tiny weight of a bit of snot. His patients would not believe how small their cavities are. No one could believe.

He presses the nerves under his eyebrows, digs in with his thumbs, but the relief is so momentary and seems only to add weight, the pain strengthened. Codeine could take care of most of it, leave him pukey and dizzy and deadened, but the pain has lasted too long. He can't take codeine for a year. At this point he can only suffer.

He pulls the string to turn out the light, a hundred beasts vanished, and climbs the stairs, pushes the door open to the apartment above. Weak light in here, yellowed, and everything seems so small.

Bed with the oldest mattress, thick and caved in the center, a back breaker. And only a single. A real trick to sleep with anyone here. No sheets on it now, only its cover, which is a pattern of pink roses, just like everything in the bathroom in the house. Windows above unable to open, suffocating in summer. Bathroom a broom closet in size, plywood painted white, essentially unfinished. But this apartment was perhaps the only place he felt true freedom. Young enough then, and though he didn't have Gary's luck, still he felt possibility, and his parents in the house could have been miles away.

He should feel freedom now, but the IRS after him is probably what kills that most. Knowing they will never stop, never forgive, never even understand that what he was doing was not supposed to be illegal. A scam for doctors and dentists in Alaska, a slick guy coming around and telling them all the tax benefits of a corporation in South America.

And it was legal at first, but then it changed, and no one bothered to tell Jim. Or maybe he kind of suspected, if he's to be completely honest, but why hand over all that money to the IRS? When was that ever something he'd agreed to? What right do they have?

If he could put the entire government on a fireworks barge and push them out into the lake and light the fuse, he would. Every rocket pointed downward so it would explode in place. He wants all of them to just die. A rage so complete there's no way to express it. Even the magnum not enough.

Jim lies down on the bed. Thick layer of dust, terrible for his sinuses, but the pain is already complete, so how can it be worse? He's moaning, because when it hits this stage there's only moaning, and thoughts no longer form or follow, and all that's left is time.

The bare light bulb humming, another torture, moth wings fusing to its surface. Too many things. Rhoda, the IRS, his divorces, the sinus pain, his job, the empty new house, winter, this trip that has not made things better at all. He was making it through the weeks until this trip, a kind of finish line, but now he can see all the weeks waiting after it, and no change, no improvement. The doctor was supposed to help. And Rhoda, and his family, seeing his kids, getting away from winter and loneliness and insomnia and work, but it's no easier here. He's no closer to seeing a way through. How to stay alive long enough to where life becomes something wanted again.

What's clear is that he can't stay another day with his parents. Two nights impossibly long. He can't get through even this one.

So Jim lies there for the next hours waiting, his back slumping, all his body getting sore in the mysterious way a bed hurts us only if we're not sleeping, and finally, long after it should have arrived, the sky through thin curtains becomes dark blue and then a lighter blue and Jim rises insubstantial, a ghost from lack of sleep, feeling the outlines of his body and outlines only. Careful down the stairs and into the house. His father already there in the bay window, sitting in his usual spot, lights off, watching the lake for signs of day.

Jim sits beside him. The water out there absolutely calm, undisturbed by any ripple or wake, blue glass. "Beautiful," he says, but of course his father doesn't say anything.

The mountains on the other side brightening at their tips and fusing. The sun a soldering gun to weld earth and sky, all turning yellow white and too hot to look at. The surface of the lake a mirror to reflect this burn, water disappearing and become only light.

His father still staring straight ahead, face lit and eyes narrowed, some scientist looking into a nuclear blast and not wanting any shielding, waiting for the shock wave and the superheated wind.

"I tried, Dad," Jim says. "I guess that's what I want you to know. I didn't just cave in. I fought for hundreds or maybe thousands of hours."

"It's not a fight," his dad says. "It's just life. You just do it."

"That's not enough reason."

"We never needed a reason."

Ripples in the light now, bright mirror become liquid again, the heat raising a wind. And a boat passing far out, dark line of its hull and wake, a fisherman out for bass.

"I don't know when a reason became needed," Jim says. "I guess that's the problem, the moment that I needed one. Who knows why that moment happened."

"The whole thing's a sack of shit. All of life. Nothing is what it was supposed to be. But you still don't end it."

Jim can't believe his father is talking. "How is it a sack of shit? Your life."

"I stab myself with insulin every day. I eat diabetic ice cream. I have no good friend left. I sit here staring out at the lake, fat as a toad. I haven't had sex in decades. I don't believe, but still I have to go to church. I know too many people in this town, and if I run into anyone at the supermarket or gas station, I have to remember the names of their kids. I was supposed to be a better father, a better husband, a better Christian, a better dentist, a better man. I grew up running traplines, and the truth is I would have liked to spend my entire life out in the woods away from people, but I had to talk with them every day and I still have to talk. I'm supposed to smile, too, but I don't think that has happened in a decade or two. Every year is only time to pass, nothing to look forward to. Heard enough?"

"Wow. Yeah."

"And I'm not talking about putting a gun to my head. I'll be here until I stop breathing, because what you're talking about is not an option."

Jim puts a hand on his father's arm. "Thank you, Dad."

"I hate everyone here," his father says. "That's the truth. I never told anyone that. I never even really thought it in a sentence in my head. But I hate all of America and everything it is. I served in the navy and so did you, but my father was

Cherokee, and we come from leaders who accommodated, who tried to make peace, and they lost everything. All was taken. They signed the treaty that led to the Trail of Tears. I spent decades here fixing everyone's teeth and talking pleasantly with them, and I could never say who I was. So everyone can burn. The whole place. The entire country."

"I had no idea."

"Yeah. That was the point. No one could have any idea what I was thinking. They still can't. I'm only telling you so you wake up. It doesn't matter if you're suffering or if your life didn't turn out the way you wanted. You continue on anyway."

"But why?"

"You don't ask that."

"And why can't we ask?"

"Look where it's gotten you. Real great, the asking."

"But the question is still there."

"No it's not."

"I have to admit I'm stunned. I've never heard you say so much."

"Well that's enough I think."

"Okay."

The lake on fire, far too bright to look at, but his father is staring anyway, his desire for immolation. A terrible choice, the worst choice, to hate every day but continue on for decades. Jim will not do that. He will spare himself that.

Jim tries to stare at the lake but it's so bright it might as well be made of aluminum. Jim remembers the fresh plates of it stacked in Oregon for the boat, oiled mirrors blinding, hot even through gloves.

Heat radiating through the window, and his father still wears that hunting jacket. He's refusing the world, refusing to blink or turn away or take off his jacket or do anything at all but suffer and stare.

"I'm not sure it matters," Jim says. "I came here to be helped, to see my family, and you just helped me. You told me the truth. You weren't absent as you've always been before, and what you said does relate directly to what I've been experiencing, the same anger, the same desire to see it all burn, the same sense of not belonging and of time as something to get through. And yet it doesn't help. It doesn't help me at all. I can see now that the trip was pointless. Even if you give me exactly what I need, it doesn't do anything."

"You don't need help. You just do your life. That's it."

"Yeah. That's the part where we're not the same. I do need a good reason. I'm not going to suffer each day just to keep on suffering."

"What did you think life was going to be? Where did you get this idea that you'd be happy?"

"Well from everyone, from everything. We've always been told that."

"No we weren't. You weren't. Not by me, at least."

"That's true."

"Stop being a baby. And stop talking about it. Just do what you need to do."

"Thanks. That's real helpful."

"It's the most helpful thing I've said. Imagine we're hunting. You're down at the bottom of The Burn or below Bear Wallow, and you decide to just not hike anymore. You don't feel like going uphill. Where does that leave you?"

"I don't think it's the same."

"How is it not the same?"

"Well if I hike I know I can get to camp, where I have a bed and food and everything else, but in real life there's no camp. We just hike uphill and the hill keeps rolling back and you find out there's more hill."

"You think too much. You forget that if you don't hike you're stuck in the brush with the sun out and no real shade and your water gone and no one there except maybe a rattle-snake or two."

"That's a better situation than what I have now."

"Self-pity. You have to stop that."

"I know. It's more dangerous than anything else. But how do you stop self-pity?"

"Like everything else, you just do."

"That's the part I'm missing."

"Then stop missing it."

"That's the same thing."

His father sighs then and takes off his baseball cap. He closes his eyes, rubs at them, and then scratches his bald head. "I don't know," he says. "I don't know what else to say."

"Thank you for trying. I mean it. I appreciate that you tried."

"Yeah." He puts the cap back and raises his eyes to the burn, and Jim knows this is as much as he'll get, the conversation over now. Is there some way he could just stop? Is there some switch inside, something activated by will? Can he listen to what his father has said and let it work?

A jet boat goes by with a skier attached, a huge curve of spray lofted every time he carves a turn. Jim always loved skiing. What if he did that every day? He could buy a boat and keep it at the green pier. Wake in the morning, talk with his dad, then go out on the water.

His father clears his throat. "I know I never say this, and that I should have said it, but I love you, son, and I don't want you to go. That's the last thing I'll say."

Jim is stunned. He's never heard this before, not once in his life. He stares into the blaze of the lake along with his father and has no idea what to say. He's been offered everything now. His father loves him, his kids love him, Gary is trying hard. Rhoda was kind to him. If he can let all of this sink in, maybe it will do something. "Thank you, Dad," he finally says. "I love you too."

That morning Jim feels a bit better. It lasts a few hours. When his mother comes into the kitchen, he's able to say hello and ask how she is.

"Oh I'm fine," she says, hugging herself in her bathrobe because the bedroom is cold. His parents have slept in separate beds since he can remember, narrow single mattresses and blackout blinds never opened during the day, the room a cave, unheated and unlit. Her bathrobe is baby blue and ancient.

She lights the stove and sets the kettle. Spoons Pero into a mug while she's waiting. Some chicory coffee substitute. The water steams and boils almost immediately, reheated twice already by his father, and she pours then adds sugar and milk. Stirs with a spoon from her station, standing at the sink and staring at the pomegranate tree and petunias and fence.

"You can come over here, Mom," Jim says. "Look at the lake."

"Oh I'm fine," she says.

"Really, how come you never get to look at the lake? How many thousands of hours have you stared at that fence?"

"Jim," she says. "You always make our lives sound so small. I'm happy looking at my garden in the morning."

"Sorry," he says. "I guess the lake is still kind of bright anyway."

"Yes. And I see it plenty every day."

"Okay, sorry."

"That's okay."

"But what are you thinking when you're standing there?"

"Oh nothing important."

"There must be some repeated things. What is it that you've thought of many times while standing there?"

"Well, I don't think anyone wants to hear that."

"I do."

His mother sighs and stares at the fence or petunias or whatever. She raises her mug to take a sip.

"I'm leaving today," Jim says.

"Today?" she asks.

"This morning. I'm going to see John Lampson and then have my appointment with the therapist in Santa Rosa at the end of the day and change my ticket to fly back to Alaska earlier."

"You don't need to do that. You can stay here."

"I can't. I didn't sleep all last night. I laid out on the pier and then in the apartment over the garage and I just can't have another night of doing that. It's too long."

"It was because you saw Rhoda. Don't see her and you'll be fine."

"Do you actually believe that?"

His mother doesn't answer, and she still hasn't looked at him.

"So last chance," he says. "What are your thoughts? What happens when you're standing there?"

"I think of a lot of things. The ladies in the church and where we'll go for lunch."

"No daily scheduling stuff. I mean other thoughts or memories."

She sighs, and her head is shaking. She obviously doesn't enjoy this at all, but he doesn't feel like stopping. He wants to know. "This is your last chance," he says. "I'll be up there in Alaska and I may not come back."

"You better come back," she says in a low voice, staring down at the sink now, or maybe at her hands.

"Tell me."

"I don't like this. But okay. I remember when the flood was up over the driveway, all water out there, and I worry sometimes. I think about my history degree. One unit short. Only one unit. Would my life be different? And I worry about you kids, all three of you. Ginny with the problems she's had in her marriage, whether Gary ever will get married, and all that's happening with you, so bright and nothing went like it should and I don't understand why. All you had to do was not destroy it. If you had just let your life happen, it would have been good. That's all you had to do, just nothing, just not get in the way."

"Thank you, Mom. It's good to know what you're thinking."

"Is that enough?"

"Yes. That's enough. Thank you."

"Because I could trot out a thousand other things if you want, memories and thoughts, all that's supposed to be mine. We're supposed to be able to have our thoughts. We're supposed to be allowed that, without being picked at."

"I'm sorry."

"Your family's not here for your entertainment. All of this is real."

"I'm sorry, Mom. It's true I just feel like prodding, since nothing matters. And it doesn't matter what you say. Dad said a lot this morning. You wouldn't have believed it. But that didn't matter either. I've hit some new stage, where everything's too late. I'll be interviewing myself now as I raise the pistol to my head. So what are your thoughts now, Jim?"

"Stop it!" she yells. She's hunched over the sink, her fists clenched at her breast, and then she leaves quickly, back to the cave of her bedroom.

"I don't know what to say to that," his father says. "You know what you're doing. And then you do it anyway."

Gary comes in. "What happened?"

"I'm just a shit," Jim says. "I upset Mom. I pushed too much. It's time to leave. We're going now to John's place, then to Santa Rosa and I'm going to see the therapist today. Then fly tomorrow. I can't stay any longer."

"We're not going today."

"Well I am, with or without you. I'm making three phone calls and then I'm splitting."

Jim goes into the dining room and grabs the green phone. He hates that it's green. He dials for the therapist and it just rings. Lazy piece of shit arriving late to work. So he asks the operator for the number of Alaska Airlines, then he's on hold and standing in the middle of this house that seems like a raft right now, something that could tilt and become unmoored. He has to get out of here.

Someone finally answers, and he's able to change his ticket to fly out tomorrow morning, connecting through Seattle and Anchorage.

Then he calls John. "I'm coming over right now," he says. "Leaving Lakeport in about ten minutes."

"You don't sound good," John says.

"I'll seem worse in person."

"Well then I look forward to seeing you soon."

"You betcha," Jim says, and he hangs up because what more is he supposed to say? Just making the last rounds. He calls the therapist again and this time gets his secretary. "Tell that miserable fuck he's seeing me this afternoon. I don't give a shit if he already has other appointments. I'm leaving for Alaska tomorrow morning and I need to see him one last time before I blow my head off."

"It's okay, Jim," she says. "Everything's okay." It's clear she's been given training for exactly this situation. He doesn't really care. He gets the appointment, which is what he wanted, and then he hangs up the green phone for the last time. He won't ever have to use it again.

He walks into the kitchen to say goodbye to his father, puts a hand on his shoulder. "Thank you, Dad. That was the best gift you could have given."

"Not too late," his father says. "You can pull it together. Don't ever think it's too late."

Gary comes in carrying his duffel bag. "Okay," he says. "I don't like this, but when has that ever mattered?"

"That's right," Jim says, and he pushes past and out the metal door and down the narrow steps a last time. All the world burning away just behind him now, vanishing. This house will be gone when he leaves, and then this road and town and lake and these mountains, all gone.

John has a nice place in Kelseyville. Big house set back from the road, old trees and plenty of shade. He owns a pharmacy and has done well. And he hasn't detonated his life at any point. His wife, Carol, comes out on the porch to join in the greeting. She's wearing a white dress with blue polka dots and a blue sash and could fit into their high school photos.

"You're a step back in time," Jim says to her. "You look like our high school dreams."

John chuckles. "That's my wife you're talking to. But yeah, you're right. The girls then did look similar."

"And she's not much older now than they were then."

"Jim," she says, smiling. "You'll have to stop that. You'll make me shy."

"Well you look beautiful," he says. "And John you have the perfect life. Look at all this."

Their son comes out the door then.

"Holy crap," Jim says. "He's even bigger now."

"Crusher," Gary says. "Definitely the biggest strongest baby I've ever seen."

"Toddler," John's wife corrects.

"Linebacker," John says. "Well come on inside. We can't just stand out here."

Inside is even nicer, the dream of a home and family, dark wood and big leather couches with John's kills spread over them, bobcats and bears, mule deer and elk. Puffy handmade throw pillows and smiling photos everywhere. His rifle, a .30-06, hung over the wide fireplace. A life built on every day repeating, every day being exactly like the last, something Jim has never been able to endure.

"Would you like lemonade?" Carol asks.

Jim is looking at the floor, made of old railroad ties sanded smooth and polyurethaned. All the knots and spike holes and lines of grain. He rubs the toe of his boot over it, Gary's boot really, and can't touch the wood. A world encased below, holding events from a hundred years, every day of the sun rising and all the rain and everything else. In an epoxy bubble like an ant in amber.

"Yes," Gary says. "We both would."

Jim sits on the couch and lies back, resting his head on bobcat, not as soft as he would have hoped. The hairs harden over time, maybe just from dust. His own hides up in Alaska all bristle now too.

The dark beams above, an open roof like in a cathedral, triangles on stout posts. "Is the wood up there old too?" he asks. "Or just stained?"

"Left rough and with about half a dozen layers of dark stain," John says. "A kind of antiquing they can do to make wood look old. They beat it up for a while, gouging and splintering the surface and maybe digging too deep with the belt sander. Like all of us in our woodworking class. We were ahead of our time."

Jim grins. "That's pretty funny. We did do some excellent antiquing without knowing."

"Lakeport's finest, to fill the castles of Europe."

"Is that what all this is, to look like Europe, like something as old as that?"

"I don't know. That or the Wild West. Must be one of the two. I guess I have no idea what we're trying to look like here."

"My whole life is like that, based on some dream but who knows which one."

"Is this where I get out my tears?"

"That's why I came to see you," Jim says. "You're the only one with a sense of humor about this. Gary is more like a grumpy nanny."

"Thanks, brother. As I go up to Alaska with you to babysit, and meanwhile leave my whole fucking life behind, I'll be happy to know it was worth it because you're so grateful."

Carol arrives with the lemonade in big glasses with pink straws.

"Where's the umbrella in my drink?" Gary asks.

"I've never even had a drink with an umbrella," Jim says. "What a sad sucky small thing I lived. I did nothing."

"Not too late," John says. "Go down to Mexico. Hang out on the beach for a while. I think you should do that right now and not go back to Alaska. Get some sun and go swimming in the ocean. Eat fresh fish and find a señorita. And because of the IRS, don't come back. Make us visit you down there."

"You're right," Jim says. "Really. That is exactly what I should do, and yet I'll be getting on that plane to Alaska."

"Is Gary going with you?"

"Yeah. I'll have to change my tickets too," Gary says. "Extra hundred bucks probably, because I'm a rich teacher who cares nothing about money. You fat cats don't care, but a hundred means something to me."

"A hundred still means something to me," John says.

"I'll pay you back for your ticket," Jim says. "And you're in my will, so you're about to get half my share of the ranch, the other half to my kids. And cash if there's anything left over after the IRS."

"They'll want everything," John says. "You have to set up a trust or they'll take the ranch."

"Maybe too late for that."

"Hey!" Gary says. "How about think for a second what you're talking about?"

"I think he knows," John says.

"That's what I like about you," Jim says. He closes his eyes and enjoys the lemonade, fresh squeezed with crystals of sugar not yet fully dissolved.

"Game of chess?" John asks.

"Yeah," Jim says, opening his eyes. "That sounds good."

This is their ritual. Sit here for a bit of chitchat then go into John's study and play one or two games for about three hours. Usually his kids are waiting here the whole time, going crazy with boredom, but this time it will be Gary.

"Entertain yourself," Jim says to him.

"I'll count my blessings," Gary says. "That should get me through a couple hours."

More leather in the study, big desk, a small chess table, a globe old-timey with ancient maps, California distorted and Alaska missing. A brass telescope. Bookshelves to the high ceiling and a ladder that slides along them. "Are you a count or a duke or something?" Jim asks John.

A wood duck mounted on the desk, prettiest of them all, blues and greens and reds.

"You've got me thinking," John says. "It's true this is supposed to be Europe. But I've never even been there."

"We have no idea why we want what we want, or who we were supposed to be."

"Do you just say those things, or do you actually think them?" John has these small round glasses that make him look smarter. Stocky build, strong, so it's hard to imagine he's been near a book, but the glasses make it seem he's some kind of natural philosopher, come in from the hunt or lumberjacking to hold forth.

"I lie awake every night," Jim says. "I sleep maybe a couple hours. Then I fall asleep again during the day. I was doing that at work, missing appointments. And all I can say about my thoughts is they're like mud, or silt, whatever might be in layers and shift around, gathered on the bottom. I get part of one and it's stuck to another, without beginning or end, and all they have is weight, finally, no shape. Imagine you dive down and grab at the mud with your hands. That's what trying to understand is like. You get all you can hold in your hands, but that's not the whole thing and isn't even a part of it, and as you come back to the surface it's all streaming away into the water. What you lift out at the end is only enough to make your hands dirty."

John smiles. "It's making you more interesting at least. You should have had your sleepless nights earlier."

"I was boring you before?"

"Let's just say you were never introspective. When I asked if you were sure about marrying Elizabeth, you wouldn't discuss it or even think about it. You had a plan, and you were doing the plan. Your whole life was like that, even when we were young, in grade school. You just always had a plan."

"That wasn't good."

"No it wasn't. The plan has worked for me, for some reason, but it never worked out for you."

"And why is that?"

"I don't know. Luck?"

Jim sits in one of the leather chairs at the chess table. He feels overwhelmed. The idea that he always had a plan, and that that was the problem. "The plan is what got me here," he says. "Having a plan, that was the problem all along, because it was never my plan. It was only what I was supposed to do."

"Seems kind of simple to blame your whole life on that. And maybe it was your plan."

"No. It's not too simple. It's the truth. The truth is always simple. I was a good person. I did what I was supposed to. But then I did what I wanted, and the two don't match."

John sits across from him and leans forward with his elbows on the table. "Then just do what you want from now on. That's simple too, right?"

Jim closes his eyes and leans back in the chair. The pain radiating and pulsing. There might be some way here, but he can't focus. "I can't let me be the bad me. I think the good me went on too long," he says. "I can kill it only by killing everything."

"Since I'm your friend, now is when I step in and say that's not true and don't do it."

"But what do you believe?"

"I believe you're going to kill yourself as soon as you get back to Alaska."

"Do you think I have a way out?"

"Yes. As easy as just taking a breath. But you won't do it. The same thing that made you valedictorian will also make you pull the trigger. You can't pull out once you head into something. You'd be disappointed now if you didn't blow your head off. It would be a failure, not accomplishing a kind of goal."

"That's crazy."

"Yes it is."

"That can't be true."

"I've never seen you not finish a plan."

All the chess pieces lined up and waiting, carved wood. The idea of making each move and thinking out all the possibilities before making the next, this just seems overwhelming, because it's what he has always done. Carefully thought about each step of his life and thought through all the consequences, and it turns out all that was wrong, the entire method wrong. "How was I supposed to think?" he asks. "If it wasn't like chess, going through and eliminating every possibility to finally make the one move that seemed to be the only safe one, what was the method supposed to be?"

"How we feel, and a bit of faith," John says. "I think that's how. But sometimes that doesn't work either."

"You're good on analysis but short on answers."

"I can't live someone else's life."

Jim feels so exhausted. He lies down on the floor, padded by carpet. "I think that was the euphoria stage," he says.

"While we were talking. That was my high. I didn't even notice it. But I just fell off the cliff. I'm miles lower now."

"Let me get you a pillow."

"Okay," Jim says, but he's still falling in waves of pain and pressure, and this is what lies underneath all the talk, this is the bedrock he's made of now, and he knows there's no hope of anything new. He knows where he's going, and the only mercy now is that he's so exhausted he may sleep.

When he wakes he's alone in John's study. Sound of rain outside, dark even though it's day. He feels some panic about what time it is and rushing to his appointment with the therapist, but he also doesn't care. His knees are sore from sleeping on the carpet, and his neck hurts despite the small pillow John brought, but the sinus pain is of course always the worst thing. Acute whenever he wakes, all the pressure built.

He rises, looking for tissue, and finds a box on the desk. Blows and it's like trying to move rocks in a quarry with a hand fan, one of those bamboo folding jobs that a lady would take to the opera. That against boulders the size of houses. Nothing is moving. He can see how surgery could start to seem like no risk at all. Just drill a hole right into my forehead. I don't care how it looks as long as everything drains.

He doesn't have his watch, and the clocks in here don't look functional. Antiques, ornamental, disagreeing on the time.

He can't get over the idea that suicide is now his plan and he won't be satisfied until he does it. John might be right about that, and understanding this might be the key to not doing it.

His head is throbbing, the inside three sizes too big for his skull, like the Grinch's heart when it grows. The casing feels like it's about to break. He sits in John's chair, heavy thick padding, and wonders what the satisfaction feels like, to be John sitting here knowing all his life is good, that everything worked out, that he can rest and simply continue on. But Jim would find it frightening, and he still doesn't know the source of that. No closer, even after talking with everyone.

Large windows, like at the therapist's, but a wider view to oaks and green grass, a small creek running through the back of the property and a hillside rising. Some nice rocks up higher. He's hiked there with John before. They brought their rifles in case they might spot a buck or an old boar.

The oaks have new leaves just coming in, bright green, a much lighter color than they'll be later. A gray squirrel bounding up onto one of the trunks and clinging there, hung sideways to the world, pausing in fear, and then another squirrel leaps up and the two chase each other around and around the trunk, going higher. So simple. Joy. Or maybe they're fighting over territory. He's never really understood what they're doing or cared. David shoots them all the time, and they're not bad eating. That's as far as Jim's interest has gone. He shot them when he was a kid, too, along with everything else. Thousands of things he's killed. All that walks or flies or swims. He should count, maybe even write it down.

He grabs a piece of John's stationery, gold embossed, suitable for a duke but missing the title, thick bond paper, and a pen. He begins at the top.

Things I have killed: Gray squirrels. He should note how many. But so hard to guess. A hundred?

"John," he calls. "Come in here."

Ground squirrels, he adds, wondering if they were supposed to have another name.

"John!" he yells again, and this time John opens the door.

"Sleeping Beauty awakes?"

"Yeah, and my dress was all bunched up. What did you do while I was sleeping?"

John chuckles. "That was Gary. Brotherly love."

"Gary!" Jim yells. "Get in here too. And take a seat John. We have an important task."

Gary walks in. "What's happening now?"

"I'm making a list of everything I've killed. I need your help."

"Why are you doing that? We need to get going."

"So I have gray squirrels and ground squirrels so far, estimated at two hundred gray and a hundred ground."

"We have to go," Gary says. "Just count the big things. Bears and moose and mountain goats."

"Okay. A little weird to list bears after squirrels, but whatever. I only killed brown bears, no black or polar, so that's easy. And I know it was only three. How many moose though?"

"About ten?"

"Maybe just list all the species first," John says. "Then fill in the numbers later."

Jim has no will, really. Any way is as good as the next. "Okay," he says.

"So you got mountain goats," Gary says. "And Dall rams. Caribou, wolverine."

"Don't mix families," John says. "Once you say caribou, we should do all the deer."

"Okay," Jim says. "Elk, mule deer, white-tails, antelope, along with caribou."

"Cats next," John says. "You got a lynx, just one, right?"

"Yeah."

"That's rare."

"Shot it right in the ass. That's all I'd ever seen, just the ass of one getting away."

"Nicest piece of ass in your life."

"True, actually. Much softer and shapelier. Having fur and having to hunt all day."

"You two are a bad combo," Gary says.

"Bobcat," Jim says. "Mountain lion. And dogs next. Coyote, timber wolf, red fox, stray dogs."

"Rabbits and jackrabbits," John says. "I've never known if there are more than two species."

"Yeah just the big ones and the small ones," Gary says. "And who cares."

"Birds," Jim says. His hand is getting sore from scribbling too fast. "Birds are going to take forever."

"Lifer," John says, and grins.

"We should have said that each time right before we shot."

"Start with ducks," Gary says. "Mallard, wood, blue, canvasback, bufflehead, ruddy, that's about all we wanted to shoot."

"But we shot others anyway."

"Yeah, I guess add wigeons, teals, mergansers, and who knows what else."

"Move on to geese," John says. "Snow geese, Canadian, and you shot emperors up on Adak, right?"

"Yeah. And sea lions, seals, and found a dead otter. Not sure whether that counts. If there's such a thing as karma, I don't know what kind of solution they'll come up with for me. No bug is low enough."

"We haven't even started on the fish," Gary says. "And you've still got so many birds: quail, doves, pheasant, grouse, turkeys, all the blue and scrub jays, flickers, random songbirds. And snakes, lizards, gophers, moles, bats, insects, maybe other things too. Ever shoot a worm?"

Jim's list is already too long. He lays his forehead on the desk. "I don't know why I'm doing this," he says. "I can't remember now why I thought it would matter."

"To take account of your life," John says. "To see how it all adds up."

"But it doesn't equal anything. Adding or subtracting a hundred birds or squirrels has no effect."

"Did you think it would?" Gary asks.

"Yeah, I did. But only a few numbers matter. Two divorces. Two kids. Two careers. Three hundred sixty-five owed to the IRS. Two nights here so far, long nights. Two men for Rhoda, and I'm not the one. Subtracted. One shot. One empty house waiting. One life and then none."

"Your life isn't math," Gary says.

"I'm so tired of talking about my life. Let's talk about your life." Jim raises his head from the desk and digs his thumb under his right eyebrow, trying to blunt the pain.

"We should go."

"No, let's hear about your life, your math. And the worst part about being you. And when you're done, it's John's turn. I want to hear."

"I don't have to do that."

"But you're going to."

Gary swings his arms, some gesture of helplessness, and sits down hard on a leather couch. How many dark leather couches are there in this house?

"Fine. I worry about money every day, can't stop thinking of it, because I can't really afford my mortgage. I think

I may sell and move somewhere cheaper, like Wyoming or Montana or Idaho. I'm taking a road trip this summer to check it out. Mary and I are going together. We'd both sell and move somewhere without traffic or crowds or hot summers or high taxes, somewhere teachers can live. It's ridiculous to try to live here as a teacher."

"Well that's good to know. How come you never told me?"

"I think your problem has kind of taken center stage."

"Sorry."

"That's okay. Just all our lives, but that's fine."

"Sorry. But what else? What else is bad in your life?"

"I didn't work hard as a student. I know I wasn't ambitious. I wanted to be a marine biologist and that didn't happen. Didn't have the grades. And I missed my chance in basketball. Maybe could have done more there."

"What else?"

"That's enough."

"No."

"Fine. I worry whether I can really stay with Mary and not want to fuck some other woman at some point. And I wish she had tits. Happy to hear all this?"

"Yeah."

"And I don't know if I ever want kids. She wants kids. And she's Catholic, expects me to maybe convert at some point, which is something I can't imagine."

"Compromise," Jim says. "You know I never did that for Rhoda. For Elizabeth either. Elizabeth had to go hunting and fishing with me even though she hated it. She was slow and I'd just leave her far behind on the trail. And she never wanted to move up to Alaska, hated it there, the endless rain and snow and nothing to do. Rhoda didn't want commercial fishing or living on a boat, and she wanted me to accept her daughter more. I didn't budge an inch with either of them. Just followed my plan. No one else's plan has ever seemed real."

"You're on to something there," John says. "You do have to compromise and pay attention to someone else's wants. It can feel good to try to make their dream happen. It feels nice to give, and you might even find you like their idea better."

"Well that's great advice five years ago, or fifteen years ago. Too late now."

"You're still here, and you'll meet someone new. Even if it takes three more wives, you still have time to figure it out."

"Thanks for that curse. Three more wives."

"I guess we're done with my story and my life," Gary says. "Typical level of interest."

"Yeah, John's turn."

"I've got no complaints."

"Well you do today. Even if you have to make them up."

"Well I can't say I find pharmacy fascinating or ever have. It's every day, for the last fifteen years, a lot of hours on my feet, kind of repetitive, more listening to complaints than you would ever imagine."

"My tooth hurts a little when I chew, or like if it gets cold, if I drink cold water."

"Exactly."

"Or at a party. Hey, you're a dentist, maybe you can tell me . . . blah, blah, blah."

"I have a new one there, if it's a party. Hey, you're a pharmacist, can you score me . . . and then fill in the blank: Demerol, codeine, whatever."

"I get that too."

"Great you two have the keys to the kingdom and can chat about all the little people. But we should go. You moved your appointment. You made it all a rush."

"Come back for summer," John says. "Stay here with us for a month or two, settle in. Some nice-looking single women around here, too, because the men are always taking off. Just hang out in the pharmacy with me for one afternoon and you'll have all the dates you ever need."

"A month or two?" Jim asks. "I must seem right on the edge. Everyone offering me too much."

"You're definitely looking over the edge at this point. And it's true it's not going to hurt, and it's going to be a relief and all that, the end of pain and worry, but it's also the end of everything, and you don't know yet what everything could be. Seems a shame."

"It's all kind of fucked anyway," Jim says.

"That's not you," John says. "Your mind has changed just recently, angry and negative, but I promise that's not you."

"Well this Future Leaders of America convention has me all choked up," Gary says.

"Yeah, I know," Jim says. "We have to go."

"One last cuddle and then say goodbye."

"Gary can make fun, but I am giving you a hug," John says, and then his arms are around Jim and Jim feels embarrassed, all too much and too fast, and he realizes this is it, the last time he'll see his friend.

"Thank you, John," he says, and he knows he's about to sink again but he looks only at the floor on the way out and that gets him through.

"We'll be passing Ukiah," Gary says. "You should see Ginny."

They're winding along a narrow creek toward the Blue Lakes, through a canyon. "I don't feel up for that."

"You never feel up for seeing her, and she notices. She's your sister. We can just say hi for fifteen minutes."

"You know she won't let us stop for only fifteen minutes. And if Bill is there, we'll have to talk with him too."

"He'll be at work."

"The answer's no." The earth here red and so many cutaways for the road. Lined with manzanita.

"Why don't you like her?"

"I never said that."

"Well why do you never want to see her?"

"Do you enjoy seeing her?"

"Not really."

"And why is that?"

"The whiny voice, I guess."

"Yeah, I've never believed her voice, our whole lives."

"Well it is her voice, like it or not."

"No it's not. It's just a fake. We've never heard her voice, except maybe when she's angry or crying. Maybe that was real."

"Well it's only one small feature. Jesus."

"That's the other problem, how religious she is. Like I want all that judgment shoveled onto me. Wheedling questions about my two divorces and about whether I'm going to church and everything pointed to whether I'm a good man, which of course I'm not."

"She's not so bad. You make her sound mean."

"She is. Always smiling, always tittering because a laugh seems more friendly, and behind all of it is pure meanness and judgment, getting out her fork and turning me over to see if the other side is roasted enough yet. Just the way she looks at me."

"She has glasses, and the lenses are thick. It just makes her eyes look bigger so you think she's examining you."

"Yeah, it's only that. You're right, little brother."

"Now who's being mean?"

They hit a flat section and then the Blue Lakes on the left. "Slow down."

Gary takes his foot off the gas and they hear the engine compression. "Want me to pull over?"

"Yeah, why not?"

They pull in under weeping willows hung down to the water. The color not as blue today, washed out by the sky. Long narrow lakes between the road and mountain. Jim gets out and walks down to the edge.

The sand rough, pebbled browns and reds and greens, a bit of blue. Water calm and clear, no one swimming at this time of year to churn it all up. Soft decay and mud only a few yards out. A rope with knots hanging, waiting. He remembers joy here, swinging on that rope with John, fighting to push each other off, endless games invented out of nothing. Gary too young, six years younger.

Small cabins all along here that you could rent, just ten by tens, enough for a bed and a bunk above. Shared toilets in the lodge. All changed now. There was in fact a different America. No drugs here then. No guns except to hunt. Almost no crime. Not just nostalgia but something lost. Now it's a dangerous place, redneck in all the worst ways instead of the best ways.

"Those six extra years," Jim says. "I saw a place you never will. All gone. Even just a six-year difference. And over the next ten or twenty, you'll see something different, too, something I couldn't guess at right now."

"We'll see them together."

"God, you sound like an after-school special, one of those crap things I'm supposed to find for David and Tracy to watch when I'm working. You wouldn't believe how bad they are, how obvious."

"Thank you for appreciating that I'm trying to help you."

"Just do it in a way that's not idiotic."

"And your thought that things change in six years is so smart. Of course they fucking change."

"Fine. I was trying to remember something, trying to remember what it felt like then, when life was a different thing entirely. But you're right. It's gone." Jim pushes the toe of his boot into the sand just behind the waterline, watches it fill and cloud. "Let's go," he says.

They climb out of this valley and descend into another and join Highway 101 and pass through Ukiah.

"Not too late to stop and say hi," Gary says.

"Too late," Jim says.

They hit Cloverdale and don't stop this time at Fosters Freeze. The world continuing to vanish behind Jim. Places that will never be seen again.

He nods off, so exhausted still, and wakes as Gary takes the turnoff in Santa Rosa.

"Almost there," Gary says. "Afterward we can see your kids again if you want."

"No."

"Why not?"

"I can't do that again. Too hard. I already said goodbye."

"It's goodbye for only a few months. You could see them again today."

Gary's denial tiring, so Jim doesn't answer. Santa Rosa so characterless, streets on a grid and just everyone living their lives. The therapist's office in a nicer section, leafier.

"Should I come in?" Gary asks when they've pulled up.

"No, I think you already have your warnings."

"Okay. Have fun."

"Should be a hoot." Jim walks past flowers expensively kept. Some famous botanist lived in Santa Rosa, a combiner of genes to make new varieties. Gardens and buildings named after him, but Jim doesn't remember his name.

"My receptionist said you talked about 'blowing your head off,'" Dr. Brown says when they're sitting. The trees in the background again, and Jim notices there's a fence beyond them, overgrown and old and hard to spot at first.

"Yep."

"Is that your plan?"

"Unless it will come off in some other way." Jim imagines unscrewing his head like a tick's. Is his head in fact burrowed

217

into something right now and he just doesn't know? That would be a real lack of perspective.

"Let's set that aside for a moment," Brown says. "We'll return. But first tell me how it was to see your family."

"Better than I would have thought. My dad actually said he loved me. And he talked for basically the first time ever. Told me all about his gripes."

"Well that's great."

"Yeah, and it didn't matter. Everyone was good to me but it doesn't matter now. I've turned some corner where it's too late."

"What corner is that?"

"The one where every question from the therapist seems idiotic. But I guess I turned that corner a lot earlier. So maybe this was a new corner."

"I'm of course not going to be hurt by whatever you say. I'm here to help you. Let's keep the focus on you. What did you feel when your father said he loved you?"

Dr. Brown is leaning forward and has his hands laced together, as if real discoveries are to be made. Jim can't look at him anymore. Far too annoying. So he closes his eyes and wonders how it felt when his father said that. There's light against his lids, leftover, slightly orange, and otherwise just darkness or nothing, and no thoughts are moving. Thoughts are only reports from far away, being sent to other people but not to Jim. "I don't know."

"Remember. Hear him say the words again. See him."

Jim tries that. He remembers pretty clearly. "I can see him. But I'm not there."

"What do you mean?"

"There's no me in the memory. No one who could have felt something, so I can't say whatever that something was."

"Open your eyes."

Jim does that. Brown looks annoyed.

"Do you want to be here, Jim?"

"No."

"Then how am I supposed to help you?"

"You can't."

"I guess we return then to your comment about blowing your head off."

"Oh that little thing."

"Yeah. I'd like to recommend a place here, instead of going up to Alaska."

"*Cuckoo's Nest* again?"

"It's nothing like that. It's terrible that movie was made. This is a place where you would have help and be safe. Right now you're not safe."

"But I am free, and I'll take that. No pills, no guards, no terrifying nurse."

"It isn't anything like that. Nurse Ratched doesn't exist in real life."

"Too bad. That's all that was keeping them alive, being able to hate her instead of just wanting to kill themselves."

"The same way you want to hate me?"

"I think you're reaching too far now. You're not important enough. You're just annoying and not very good at your work."

Jim can see that this hits. Only for a moment, but Brown has some sort of professional pride. "Right there," Jim says. "That's the problem. You're not supposed to reveal any of you. But I can see you and your limits."

"I'm human, not a machine. And I'm trying to help you."

"Then you should have helped me. When I first arrived, I was willing, but you had one eye on the clock and the other on your wallet."

"You're angry that you can't find a way out of your despair, and I understand that. And it's okay to blame me. But we need to do the real work now. Who is it in you asking for help right now? What does that Jim feel like?"

"Is this one of those child self and six other selves things? Because all that is crap. There's no self, no Jim, and certainly no group of Jims in here. And yeah my moods go up and down but I don't become different people. There's just the world stretching endlessly but empty, like tundra up in Alaska. It goes on and on, and that's what it's like inside, a wasteland you'd never be able to cross, only wind. Pressurizing at every edge but just nothing in the middle. So what I need is either a way to remove the pressure, so that it's okay to wander endlessly in nothing, or I need there to be something on that tundra, someplace to shelter or hide or go into and make a life. One of the two. But wandering around in nothing under pressure is not something I can endure. I can't keep doing that for years."

Dr. Brown is sitting back now in his chair, looking thoughtful. "That's good, Jim. That's a good description. Thank you."

"You're welcome. That'll be sixty dollars."

Brown's smile is only a wince. "I want you to close your eyes now. Close them."

Jim is reluctant but does it.

"Now imagine that tundra, that empty open space."

"Not hard. It's always here."

"Now imagine yourself walking along, and I want you to see a cabin."

"That's never there, but okay."

"Let's make it something else then. Are there mountains?"

"Yes. At the edges."

"Can you see a cave there?"

"Yeah there are caves."

"Okay, walk into one of those caves. Find one big enough to be comfortable."

Jim can see tundra in the fall, when the blueberry has turned and there are so many colors, shades of red and yellow and green, and the mountains all snowcapped. A bull moose at the edge of one of the million small lakes and mosquitoes everywhere in dark clouds that shape-shift constantly. He's following one of these and approaches the base of a cliff, and there's a cave, cut like an eye into the rock, and when he steps inside it's much larger than it looked. Dark ceiling with shapes hanging down, slick floor like the skin of a halibut, mottled green and brown. "The floor is the topside of a halibut," Jim says. "I'm standing on its skin, and the cave is very cold, as cold as the ocean bottom."

"A halibut? The fish?"

Jim tries to ignore Brown, who is fucking up the vision. The chamber he's found feels sacred, the home of his totem animal, and maybe there could be some answer here. He walks over the slippery flesh and looks for the rise of gills, for the slow breathing.

"What do you see?"

"Just shut up," Jim says, and he tries to breathe this air in the cave, wondering if it's water, if he's submerged, and he can see only shadows, without shape. Everything so dark. He's walking with his hands out, and step after step brings him no nearer to anything. The cave extends as far as the ocean floor and is as featureless.

"I'm just going to wander," Jim says. "There's nothing to find. I picked a totem animal who lives in a place unlivable. Under the pressure of ten atmospheres, and no light, and no solid ground, only mud that stretches for thousands of miles without feature. That's exactly what the inside of my head is like. The pressure, the darkness, the lack of solid ground, the lack of feature or distraction or any other relief, just stretching on forever, and the thing is, I can't do forever." Jim can feel himself choking up at the thought of having to endure. Feeling sorry for himself again. "And now I'm fucking crying again about poor me having to face forever."

"It's okay. Don't be hard on yourself."

"I'm a fucking baby. There's nothing wrong and I still fall apart."

"Sometimes we think mental illness is nothing, but it's something, and you're suffering, but you can get past it and recover and be yourself again. It's possible."

"You haven't been here. If you had seen this place you'd know."

"Keep your eyes closed and keep walking. Can you do that for me?"

"Yes." Jim keeps walking farther along the bottom.

"And now I want you to stop and turn around and find the light from where you entered."

Jim opens his eyes. "That's just so stupid. Honestly. The light at the end of the tunnel? Come on."

"Sorry," Brown says. "Maybe it was too obvious."

"Yeah. I told my kids they took a halibut up to the moon and let it fly, but I'm realizing now that the moon is an easy place, so much nicer. So much easier to live there."

"Are you going to see your kids again today?"

"No. Just going to the airport and then up to Fairbanks."

"And your brother is still going with you?"

"Yes."

"I need to talk with him again."

"Honestly? I think he's been briefed. And I'm not a child. So no, you don't get to talk with him."

"Okay. Well we need to come up with a plan."

"No we don't. The plan was the problem all along."

"What's that?"

"Talking with my friend John, I realized I've always had a plan, and that's been the problem. He thinks killing myself is my plan now, something I have to accomplish, like finishing my homework, and I can never not finish my homework."

"So it has to be okay to fail at this idea of killing yourself."

"Yes, even though that's embarrassing."

"Embarrassing?"

"Yeah, everyone expects it now. And I've told everyone. Would be awkward to stick around."

"That's interesting. So how can we make it okay to fail at this?"

"Just undo all my education and everything I've been for almost forty years."

"Maybe you could write a letter to yourself, explaining why it is you can't do it and why that's going to be okay."

"Sixty just seems like too much. You need to think about your rates. Writing a letter to myself? Dear Jim, where did all the happy thoughts go? Why can't we go skipping through the corn again? PS: I'm not going to be able to pull the trigger. Sorry, but don't be mad."

Dr. Brown is looking down at his hands now. Jim has broken him just a bit, maybe. "It feels good to break you," Jim says. "A bit of unexpected satisfaction right at the end. So thank you for that."

Jim counts out three twenties and walks quickly around the desk. Brown puts up his hands to protect his face, some instinctive reaction, but Jim reaches down quick and tucks the money into the waist of his jeans. "Thanks for fucking me."

Brown looks angry but Jim is laughing, this rush of happiness, buoyant, and he walks out. He will never see any therapist's office again.

Gary is waiting in the truck. "What?" Gary asks. "What's so funny? Why are you smiling? And why are you done early?"

Jim gets in the passenger side and just feels better. "I feel good," he says. "We had a kind of breakthrough. It all feels lighter now."

"Really?"

"Yeah."

"Well that's great! That's fantastic."

"Yep. I've turned a corner. I'm no longer afraid to go back up to Alaska." Jim looks at Gary, both of them grinning, and Jim thinks this is perfect. This is the way it should go. "You don't even need to come up. You can continue on with your teaching and Mary and not have the disruption."

Gary looks wary at that. "But I'm not supposed to leave you alone, especially during these first two weeks on the medication, and I'm supposed to keep you away from your guns."

"Brown said that's not necessary anymore. He said I don't have to be watched."

"How is that possible?"

"It's a different understanding. I realized, from talking with John, that suicide was my plan, a kind of thing I felt I had to accomplish, and now I see I don't have to do that."

"Wow."

"Yeah."

"Well let me think about this." Gary starts the truck and drops it into drive and they ease away.

Jim isn't sure what to say next. He needs to be careful not to say too much. All his life he's known that believability depends on fewer words. A little liar right from his earliest memories. So when he lied to Elizabeth and to Rhoda he was doing only what came naturally. It never seemed wrong.

"We also had a breakthrough about the guilt," he adds, unable to hold back. He loves the lies and finds it very hard to stop. "It's an engine for the self-pity. I understood that for the first time today. I beat myself up so much, all the time, and then I feel sorry for myself."

"Wow. This is all new," Gary says. "And so quick. What a session."

"Yeah the therapist was great. He pointed out that wanting to sleep with other women is only natural and actually I didn't hurt anyone."

"Hm," Gary says.

"Yeah, I know. You don't agree."

"I think it's better you're thinking of it this way," Gary says. "Really. And Elizabeth and Rhoda are both fine."

"Yeah, infidelity is not doing anything bad to anyone. It's just doing something good with someone else and not telling the truth about it. But even not telling the truth is okay, because no one wanted the truth."

"Well," Gary says, but then waves his hand in the air. "I'm sorry. I can't help myself. I'm glad you had a good session, and I'm glad you found a new way of thinking."

Jim is surprised to find out Gary has judged him. In his head, the idea that his family was judging him was only a story, and he suspected that actually they were being easier on him. So strange.

Jim looks out his side window for some privacy and wonders how anyone's head makes any sense. He catches glimpses of himself whenever something dark passes. A face in lumps, too old and slack for thirty-nine. Lump of his chin, lump of his cheek, forehead sticking out too far, hair curly light brown and not belonging, eyes hidden away in shadow.

"Sorry," Gary says. "This is great, really."

Jim can't afford to sink right now. He has to remain upbeat and seem repaired, all fixed. "We should have a good dinner," he says. "Celebrate. It'll be my treat, wherever you want to go. Then I'll get a hotel and you can go back up to Sebastopol."

"I don't know," Gary says. "I promised everyone I wouldn't leave you alone."

Jim puts his hand on his brother's shoulder. "It's alright now. They'll understand. If you want me to call Mom and Dad and explain, I will."

Gary grins. "Okay, okay. Let's just have dinner and we can talk about it later."

The sun is going down as they approach the bay. All the houseboats next to the highway, one of them a mini Taj Mahal. Buoys and dinghies and other floating crap, everything jammed in close, too many people, and the hills the same, houses on top of each other. All the free land farther north.

The highway sweeping up into final hills before descending to the Golden Gate, veins of red and white lights. The feeling of emptiness at the edge as they cross over. Jim would like to jump. Much more dramatic and tragic, and not violent, maybe easier for his kids. And a better story. He could go head first, make sure, because sometimes people survive the jump and live on as vegetables.

That's one thing he worries about, shooting himself in the head and then living. But it's unlikely with a .44 magnum. It really should take off most of his head. He hasn't decided mouth or temple. Or just tucked under his throat and pointing upward. No information about what method is best. He can't ask anyone.

All the traffic on Lombard slow, and he feels impatient. He shouldn't have to put up with traffic at the end. "Fucking traffic," he says.

"Yeah, life turns to shit in cities."

"Life turns to shit everywhere," Jim says, but then he remembers he has to be positive. "But I'm feeling so much better now. It's amazing. Like a weight gone."

"It's so fast," Gary says.

They pass through the Mission District again, mostly Mexican. His dad never able to say he was Cherokee. Jim had no idea what his father was thinking all those years. No idea at all. "Do you know Dad hates America?"

"What? He doesn't hate America."

"Yes he does. Deeply and completely, everything it is and everyone here. It explains a lot about his behavior over the years."

"That's not true."

"He said it this morning."

"No he didn't."

"Fine. Enjoy your denial. Why does anyone bother talking with you?" But then Jim remembers again he's supposed to be fixed and nice now. "Sorry," he says. "I realize it's hard to believe, because he didn't say anything before. But it's true."

"Wow. He said that?"

"Yes."

"But why? Why hate America, and why say something now if not before?"

"Now because I'm on the edge, of course. Everyone going the extra mile for me. And he hates everyone because he could never say he was Cherokee. Had to be friendly and talk with everyone while knowing they'd look down on him or worse if they knew who he was. So nothing was real for his whole adult life in Lakeport, his whole career as a dentist, and even in his retirement when he has to keep saying hi to all his former patients."

"It's just hard to believe."

229

"Then don't believe it. I'm not sure it matters one way or the other. Nothing can be done. He's already lived a shitty life and will keep living a shitty life."

"No. It was a good life. We had good times, hunting and fishing and living on the lake."

"Yeah, he liked it when we were on the ranch and hunting. That's the only time he liked, I think."

"We're talking about him like he's gone, but he's still here, and he can make changes if he's not happy."

"He can't and he won't, and I understand why. Momentum, same as in my life. Doesn't matter if you know what's wrong or that there could be another way. You're still stuck on the path, just because you've been on it for too long. Nothing changes that."

"But you just changed today."

"True. So yeah, you're right, momentum doesn't rule all." Jim has to pay more attention. "So Dad could maybe loosen up."

They're shitted out the southern end of the city, the worst neighborhoods, all slum and industry, and drive along the water past the airport to an area with hotels. "Anything's fine," Jim says. "Any hotel." So Gary picks and Jim checks in and then they're standing at the elevator and Gary is having second thoughts.

"I'll get my bag," Gary says. "I need to stay with you. I need to be on that flight tomorrow."

Jim sets his bag down and puts his hands on Gary's shoulders, like some preacher taking one of the flock. "Gary. I'm okay now. Still not that fun to talk to, and still not that happy with how my life has gone, but I no longer need to kill myself, okay?"

Gary can't look at him for long. Younger brother, swayed all his life by Jim. Now will be no different. Momentum. We can never break free.

"Okay," Gary nods. "I'll drive back home after dinner."

"Thank you." Jim hits the button for the elevator again. "I'll be right down. Maybe ask about restaurants. Let's celebrate with something good."

The elevator is about as lonely a place as you can imagine, bare stainless box cutting off the world and erasing movement, but the room is even worse, old carpet and cheap plywood with a view out to a wall. Jim sets his valise on the desk, takes out the magnum. He sits in front of the crappy little mirror and puts the pistol to the side of his head. Loaded, so not much effort is required. Why bother to travel all the way to Alaska?

He looks old, his skin pale and slack. And the baggy clothing from Gary. This is the worst he's looked in his entire life, which makes sense of course. No suicide is looking good in his final moment.

The problem is that everything is chronic, not acute. The pain in his head the same as on other days, his despair the same, the feeling of sinking and regret and guilt and self-pity and anger. But not enough to make that trigger pull. He could drift in this region forever, which is the most frightening thought, far scarier than death.

So he puts the pistol back in his valise and zips it and returns to Gary.

"Powdering your nose?" Gary asks.

"Something like that."

"Sounds like an Italian restaurant is our best bet. Right near here."

So they go there and it's big. A bus pulled up outside. The kind of place senior proms and tours go. Satiny slips on the chairs, bows and ribbons everywhere, a pig dressed like a princess.

"Looks good," Gary says, and Jim wonders if he really doesn't see.

"Great," he says, and he knows already they'll be ordering the chicken parmesan, which will account for about sixty percent of the orders here. But there's no point in getting grumpy about a restaurant. The Last Meal, or is it the Last Dinner? Suddenly he can't remember. Last Supper. His brain is just not working.

They're seated near a big family with kids climbing on the table to reach for each other, shouting. "Fucking eh," Jim says.

"We can go somewhere quieter if you want," Gary says, barely audible.

Jim shakes his head. He can't shout. And maybe this is better, not having to talk in the end. It seems perfect, actually, to have everything blotted out by the dumbest noise. He looks at the menu and decides chicken cacciatore instead of parmesan.

"Wine?" Gary shouts.

Jim shakes his head again. He never liked alcohol. Never liked most of what everyone likes. Only sex.

Gary stands up. "We're moving," he says, indicating the door. He gives a look at the family, who don't notice, of course, and then they're outside where the bus is idling, bathed in diesel exhaust, and Gary is looking up and down the street. "Burger joint," he says. "Perfect."

"Fancy," Jim says.

They walk an unlit portion of sidewalk, just bare roadway along a construction site, the kind of place in a city where you could be mugged, and Jim wishes that would happen. But they make it safely to the diner, an old place smelling of deep-fry.

The menu is written on the wall behind the counter. The bacon burger finally. Jim feels a momentary joy. "Extra barbeque sauce," he says. "Extra bacon."

"I'll get the same," Gary says. "Sounds good. And a chocolate shake."

"Chocolate banana malt," Jim says.

"Yeah, change mine to that too."

The guy behind the counter is mute. Only a head nod and the total showing on the register. Jim pays and is handed a number on a metal stand.

They sit at a table in the corner, mashed up close to others. Blue paint, very thick, and the concrete beneath them painted the same blue. As if someone just grabbed a can of paint and hurled it at this area. "You know where to take a girl," Jim says.

Gary laughs. "Yeah, pretty nice. Worth it to come all the way to the big city for this."

Jim grins.

"Hey I'm happy you're back," Gary says. "Nice to see a smile."

Jim knows not to extend it too long. It'll look fake then. He feels the terror of what to talk about next. How to fill the time between now and whenever Gary leaves. And after that he's going to get fucked. He's going to find a prostitute here.

"What are your plans for Fairbanks?"

Gary looks so hopeful, seems to believe Jim has turned a corner, and this is the perfect intro for a liar. Plans can balloon endlessly and never need proof. "I'm going to swim more again," Jim says. "At the university pool. That always relaxes me. And take a diving class. I saw they have those. Learn the high dive properly."

"That sounds great."

"Yeah, and more cross-country skiing, on the university course. The nice thing about Fairbanks is how much sun we get in the winter. It's cold but almost always sunny. So most days are beautiful for skiing." He almost says Gary should see it, but realizes that's a mistake. He can't provide any reasons for Gary to come up.

"This all sounds positive," Gary says. "Keeping yourself busy and enjoying what's good about the place."

"There's one other thing I'm excited about. They have an opening in a barbershop quartet."

"You would love that!"

"Yeah, it's been so long, and I do love it. I played a bit of trumpet for the local theater, but that was a while ago, my last time onstage."

"You can wear a straw hat and the red-and-white stripes."

"Yep. One of the guys is a doctor I know." Jim is reaching now. Somehow he's managed to not make any friends up there, and Gary might remember this.

But Gary doesn't notice, and their order comes quickly, the chocolate banana malts so good all either of them can do is moan. The burgers piled with bacon and barbecue sauce, the real thing, served with onion rings. Jim takes a huge bite and closes his eyes and thinks this could be the way through.

Just go for simple pleasures. You don't pull the trigger when your mouth is full of bacon. No one would do that. "Bacon," he says. "Bacon."

"Yeah."

"What have been the best things in your life, the things you've enjoyed most?"

Gary opens his eyes, says "God this is good" with his mouth full.

Jim waits for him to finish chewing.

"Well," Gary says. "Speed skiing. Even though it terrified me and I stopped right away, I did enjoy that."

"How fast were the jet boats going?"

"Ninety."

"Holy crap."

"And basketball. I always loved basketball. Not sure why, but something about being on a team. The best experiences are in a group or on a team."

"I haven't done that enough."

"You've missed something there."

Jim wonders about this. An isolated life. How did he miss the group? He's given zero importance to anything social.

"And commercial fishing with you," Gary says. "That was something. Being out there, and also building the boat."

"Thank you."

"Yeah, that was great. I don't know what else. Sex of course, but that's number one on any man's list. Food some-times. The piles of abalone we've had. That's going to get more and more rare."

Jim can see he's had a good life, rich. He's had everything Gary's had, except the sports and more social life, but he's also had more money and opportunity. Somehow he didn't make use of all of it, though, or didn't find it to be enough, and it's a mystery why.

The grainy malt in the chocolate shake, a pleasure that should by itself be enough reason. The ripe banana too. His brother who loves him, who's happy and relieved that Jim is well. That trusting and easy.

They finish the burgers and shakes and just sit stunned for a while. Fresh burgers brought out to other patrons, and even when he's stuffed they still look good.

"Well," Jim finally says. "You should maybe hit the road, so you don't get up there too late."

"Yep," Gary says. "Are you sure you're going to be okay?"

"I'm fine now."

"I'm happy to come up, even for just a couple days to be sure."

"I know, and I appreciate that. But there's no need now. I feel good. I just enjoyed a burger and shake with my brother, and I feel normal. I'm looking forward to things up in Fairbanks and I'm also thinking of what you said about basketball. That barbershop quartet is my chance for a new group of guys, and I'm going to enjoy that and see what's possible."

"You're on the right track there. You'll get a lot from that."

"I think so." Jim nods then and raps his knuckles on the table and they stand. Out of the blue world of the burger joint and along the crap construction site again. Jim has an eye out for prostitutes but doesn't see any yet. He'll have to ask the doorman or the bellboy.

In no time at all they're standing in the hotel parking lot by Gary's truck. Jim's last moments with his brother. He feels this overwhelming sadness and loss but can't show it, so he smiles and gives Gary a hug. "Thank you, brother," he says. "Thank you for doing so much for me."

"Hey, that's all right," Gary says. "Just happy you're back."

"Come up fishing this summer. Some new spots on the river I've heard about for kings."

"God, I'd love to. But no money, and I think we're doing that road trip to look for somewhere else to live."

"I'll pay for your flights. Just think about it. Catching a seventy-pound king in a river, like the fattest trout you've ever seen."

Gary laughs. "That does sound good."

Then Gary is in his truck and starts it, rolls down his window to wave goodbye, and is gone. Jim's last lifeline, last moment with anyone who cares for him. Alone now. But no longer having to smile, no longer having to lie. He's going to fuck his way into exhaustion and then pull the trigger and be done. To hell with this life.

The hotel doorman looks a bit afraid, or maybe Jim is only imagining it. But maybe Jim looks that grim. It's possible. "I want a prostitute," Jim says. "Small and young. I want beautiful. I don't give a shit about disease, and I'm not using a condom."

They're standing outside the glass doors, no one around at the moment.

"I'm sorry, sir," the doorman says. "But prostitution is illegal in California."

"I'm not police," Jim says. "And here's fifty for you for finding me a couple good ones. I want one now and another a couple hours from now. Maybe a third later. I'm willing to pay for the best you know of."

"I see," the doorman says. "What room are you in, sir?"

So the arrangement is made, and Jim won't have to wander the street like a jackass not knowing where anything is. He showers, looks at his dick a small limp thing, sad, and hopes it will go up when the time comes.

He dries off hard, wanting to get rid of old skin, then sits in bed naked under the covers and watches an old episode of *Gilligan's Island*, wishes he could have Mary Ann, misses Rhoda so badly he could howl.

He's into an episode of *Hogan's Heroes* before there's a knock.

When he opens the door, she walks right in. Small and thin with black leather pants and heels. Looking obviously like a prostitute, but apparently the people at reception don't care, which is good.

"I'm not cheap," she says. "Can you afford me?" She's so cute and young. Pale skin and long dark hair.

"I'll pay," he says.

"Three hundred."

"What does that include?"

"Thirty minutes of anything you want."

Jim reaches into his pocket and pulls out six fifties. He walks up close and she takes them, tucks them into her purse. "No kissing, though," she says.

"And no condom," Jim says.

"I know. I was told."

She walks over to the desk to dump her purse and jacket. Her shirt is red leather and covers only her chest, her midriff and shoulders exposed. Jim touches her lower back, the skin so soft. She's certainly better than any woman he's ever been with.

"Take a shower," she says.

"I just did."

"Do it again."

Jim wonders if she'll steal. He grabs his wallet and valise with the pistol, closes the bathroom door and locks it. She could leave with his three hundred and he'd have no recourse. He's not sure what holds any of this together.

He picks up the pistol and holds it in the mirror. Only man and pistol, Limp-dick Jim ready for his last stand. But he puts the pistol away, zips the bag closed, and takes his shower.

When he emerges she's lying back against the pillows, her heels still on. Looking comfortable, though. All strangely normal, as if they're really a couple sharing this room.

He walks close and drops the towel. "Sorry," he says. "You look good, but it's not going up."

"Leave it to me," she says. "Just lie down."

She moves over and he lies back against the pillows. The room a bit cold but not too bad. He watches as she licks one of his nipples, which feels good but isn't giving him a boner. He's so worried now about whether he can get it up. His last hurrah, so it had better work. He's not willing to go out on total failure.

She kisses his stomach and then his thighs and takes him in her mouth and still nothing. And she has this angelic face, so perfect, and big breasts in red leather. He doesn't know what else she could possibly offer.

She pushes his legs apart, and he says no, but she goes slowly lower, soft kisses and gentle licks, and he goes up. She doesn't stop. Strokes him lightly with her hand while she licks, and she's watching him. He loves seeing her eyes while she does this.

She seems to know how easy it would be for him to lose it. She's taking her shoes and pants off while she has him in her mouth, going all the way down, swallowing him, and she's up in one quick movement so there's no time to go soft, riding him and taking off her top. She has by far the nicest body he's ever seen. He knows she cares nothing for him, but he's grateful anyway that she's so good at what she does. This is close enough to feeling loved. She even smiles and kisses his neck.

Afterward Jim takes another shower and rests but is afraid to sleep. He has to hear the next knock when it comes. He doesn't know why he didn't see more prostitutes earlier. Better dates than he would ever be able to get, and in return he gives money, which means nothing to him anyway.

He feels exhausted already, from the last couple days and lack of sleep and now from sex. He keeps thinking of Rhoda, so he calls her.

"How are you, Jim?" she asks, and it sounds embattled, like she's getting ready for the long trudge. He doesn't want her voice to sound like this. And he realizes she could call Gary so easily, so he can't tell her the truth today.

"Much better," he says. "A breakthrough with the therapist, and also when I visited John, so I feel okay now."

Pointless conversation, and he ends it quickly. He'll have to call her from Alaska, when it's already too late and no one can stop him.

The knock comes earlier than he expected, business moving right along. She's small and young also, with blonde feathered hair, wearing leather, a black jacket with golden zippers. But he feels only exhausted, not excited at all. "I

can't," he says. "Here's three hundred, and tell the doorman no more." He hands over the bills, which she takes without saying anything.

He closes the door, lies down naked on his back on the floor, the cold tiles, and wants Rhoda, wants to go back to the time when she loved him, when all was innocent, before he cheated. In his office, after hours, when they'd darken one of the rooms and she'd hold his face and give him the most tender love.

The night another without sleep, a wasteland to cross. He's walking the streets all the way to the airport, which is quiet now, no planes moving. He stands at the fence and looks at open runways, vast stretches you could walk forever, trailing into the ocean and more darkness, and the tails of planes all huddled around the terminals, shark fins waiting.

He would climb the fence and wander the runways but there's razor wire. He wants open space, without clutter. That was the point of Alaska. Fairbanks on a flatland stretching hundreds of miles, interrupted only by rivers. He might take his cross-country skis and just go. Ski all day and into the night and never turn around, and then it won't be clear there was ever a suicide. His body might not even be found. Such empty places, endless thin paper birch trees. At sixty below, he won't last even through the day, probably. Won't have to suffer another night. This is far better than the pistol, and freezing to death is easy. He'll feel warm in the end and won't understand a thing, won't even know he's dying. Easiest way possible.

The road he's on now lined with Dumpsters, and the pavement wet from rain. Cold but not cold enough for snow or anything clean. Runoff of waste and trash and too many people, every airport and city a sore. He's always hated them. No ground he can touch here, no grass, no tree, not a single living thing. Only back lanes leading to nothing, service roads.

The garbagemen are the first to join him. Driving as if using a stick for the first time, jolting and stopping over and over and dragging metal across pavement, making the most outrageous noises, no effort at all to be quiet. The sky starting to hold light, and the first jet engines spinning up and roaring off over the water. Jim can't see them from where he is now. He should have planned better. He's cold and exhausted and so hungry and thirsty.

He returns to the hotel for the breakfast buffet, has to hang around another forty-five minutes waiting, and then it's only continental, which has always disappointed everyone. Europeans are supposed to like it, but is that possible? He chews through cold rolls with jam and butter and thinks it should be better in the end. If they knew, they would make more effort.

He takes the shuttle to the terminal and does more waiting. How much of his life was waiting?

All these people around him, and he has no connection with any of them. He could vanish and it would all be the same. When he boards the plane, also, he sits next to a stranger who will remain a stranger, and it was never any different, really, in the rest of his life except for his kids and wives and family, just that small handful.

He's so tired he falls asleep on the first flight, then feels groggy going through the Seattle terminal, tries not to fall asleep while waiting for the Anchorage flight. He doesn't want to miss it. He has a plan to finish, his assignment, his homework. Those words seem different now. It was everything that happened related to home that brought him to this point, and it does feel assigned rather than chosen.

He sleeps on the Anchorage flight, too, wakes at the end to see coastline and islands, beautiful from above. Only scattered clouds. Glaciers and ice fields looking so soft. He should do something spectacular, go skydiving and not pull the cord. Go for the highest dive possible and enjoy what time there is.

At this altitude, humanity is erased. No sign of any building or boat, mountains miniaturized, waves flattened, the world innocent. He could live in it from this far view, if he never had to come any closer. The inland waterways especially idyllic, small blue mirrors and always calm.

He waits again in Anchorage, so much smaller, and cold even inside. His big jacket on now, thermal underwear and boots. He has to walk outside to board the plane, and he wonders what happens to someone who didn't know, just passing through from some tropical place, wearing shorts and flip-flops. Do they die of exposure? But everyone seems to know, all wearing parkas like his, gloves and hats and snow boots.

A plane with props and seating for less than twenty, and not much warmth, thin walled. All sitting in their full gear. It does feel like they're going somewhere wrong, somewhere close to the edge of the world. Billions of people but you'd never believe it here.

The plane so light it's thrown constantly by turbulence, sinkholes in the air, sudden drops, and yawing side to side, as if refusing direction. And dark, always dark, though now, in mid-March, sunset isn't until after 7:30 p.m., which is fine. It's only the middle of winter that gets really depressing, and he's past that now. No excuses. He can blame only himself, not the place.

They pass countless mountains unseen, Denali out there somewhere on the left an enormous white mound dwarfing normal ranges, and then the few lights of Fairbanks below and they're landing.

No one to greet him at the airport, and it's late, almost eleven. He's managed to set up a life here completely alone. It was never his plan, really. We don't make plans and don't follow plans. That's only an idea.

His truck has been plugged in the entire time he's been away, a heater keeping the engine from freezing, and this strikes him now as tremendous waste, since it's only fourteen below at the moment, but everything up here is like that, and the pipeline erases all concern. Boom times. So much like a western, all the men who have come here for a black gold rush. Fairbanks even has saloons, which is where he should go now. Why go home?

He unplugs the truck and starts it and crawls away on studded tires. Everyone moving slowly, the roads packed snow. Jim heads downtown to a saloon where he knows there are prostitutes. He's not going to waste time looking.

The walls made of logs, and inside there are peanut shells on the floor. Small round tables, two dancers on stage. Warmer in here for them, so he has to shed his jackets and wishes he didn't have the thermal underwear. Sweating already.

One of the dancers looks pretty good. A body never seems real in this light. It looks made out of wax. But still he enjoys the show. The waitress, topless and young, asks what he'd like.

"You," he says. "I know you're not a prostitute and don't usually do it, which is why I'm asking. How about five hundred bucks if you go upstairs with me for twenty minutes?"

She has long dark hair pulled back tight in a ponytail. Slim and new and busty.

"Five hundred?"

"Yes. A one-time offer, right now."

"Okay," she says. "But you owe another fifty to the bar, for the room and my time."

"I'm fine with that."

"Cash right now."

Jim pays. He's been carrying a lot of cash, but there's so much more in his account. All unused, and it will be taken by the IRS. He should buy a hundred rounds of drinks and have everyone toast to "Fuck the IRS." No Alaskan likes taxes or the government. He wouldn't find a single dissenter.

He follows her upstairs. The room is meant to look like the old West. Rough plank flooring and walls, stained dark, a four-post bed with a satiny red cover that says brothel, and oil lamps. A spittoon in the corner. He doesn't have the magnum with him, and no belt and holster for it, either, or he would hang that around one of the bed posts.

She stands in front of the bed, and it's clear she doesn't really know what to do. She's not asking him to shower.

He walks up close and puts his hands on her breasts, cool skin from working bare, a bit clammy. He can smell her sweat. She lets him run his hands along her back and belly, then he unbuttons her cut-offs and lets them fall. Wearing granny underwear beneath, just pale beige and full fitting, so he pushes those down quick and tries to forget the stains on the crotch.

He pushes her onto the bed and spreads her legs but she just looks and smells too womanly and real.

He unbuttons his jeans and pulls them down a bit and stands there limp.

"You're not even hard."

"I know. Sorry."

She sits up and leans in to take his dick in her mouth dutifully, and they could be married, the feeling of obligation without any real desire left. He watches her pretty face, because it should turn him on to see her doing this, but his dick is so loose and blank and he's feeling no pleasure at all.

"Never mind," he says. "Just lie down and I'll get behind you."

She turns away from him on the bed and he finishes stripping, lies down behind, spoons her. A bit cold in here, and they're on top of the satiny cover instead of underneath. He knows he'll never get an erection again. He can feel his time ticking away.

"What are we doing?" she asks.

"Shh," he says. "Let me just hold you. You feel good. I know it's only twenty minutes. I know my time's up soon."

He breathes in the smell of her hair and neck, her sweat, feels grateful for something real in the end. He closes his eyes, pulls her as close as he can, and tries not to feel alone, but it's only moments before he's starting to weep. He tries to keep from moving or making any sound, but she can tell.

"You're crying?" she asks.

"Sorry," he whimpers.

"This is too weird," she says, prying his hands away.

"Please. Please just five more minutes. Let me hold you."

She relaxes then and he no longer has to hide. He holds her and his body is shaking and face drowning. The crying comes in heaves that he feels from far away, like watching waves crash on some other shore.

She does something unexpected then. Turns toward him and takes him in her arms, holds his head against her breast, mothering him, a bit of generosity. "It's okay," she says. "It's okay." She doesn't get up to leave but stays a long time just like that, her hand stroking the back of his head and neck, his face wet and buried in her breasts. He's been surprised so many times now by generosity, by all that everyone is doing for him, even this stranger.

But he wrecks it, of course. "What if I offered to marry you," he says. "Right now. I'd sign something that says you get everything, my house and business, all my cash, if we ever separate or if I die. I'm a dentist. You'd be safe financially, and if you held me like this, I'd be safe also. I can tell you're a good person, generous. It's all I need to know."

"I just wanted to help you," she says, letting go of him and sitting up. "Because you seemed sad."

"Yes, and I appreciate that."

"I don't want to marry you. Jesus. I have a life."

"Sorry."

"You don't just offer to marry someone, like buying a sandwich."

"Sorry."

She's pulling on her shorts, and there's no shirt to put on, so she's out the door quickly. He knows she won't talk to him again when he gets downstairs. A bouncer will intervene or something. She'll be giving everyone warning right now.

He lies back down and closes his eyes. Desperation is truth. He would in fact be lucky to marry her, and she would be better off having the security. He's going to kill himself now, and she's going to struggle through shitty relationships with younger men and not have enough money. She should have taken his offer.

All that's left now is to go home. It will be his last drive. He gets up and walks downstairs knowing these are the last people he will ever see, all strangers. The girl hidden away somewhere, of course, and the other girls and bouncers looking at him, just as he thought. The customers oblivious. Old men at the bar, far older than he is, worse lives no doubt, and yet they are managing to carry on, even though they're probably drunks. Fat or too skinny, with destroyed noses.

A young guy at one of the round tables, a woman on each side of him. He's chomping on peanuts and tossing the shells. Dark mop of hair and face too round, young enough to still have zits, and where did he get his money?

But no one's story matters now. Jim pulls on his parka, steps back into the cold and dark and crunches across the snow, the music muted. He climbs in his truck and drives out of town on a road that hasn't been plowed. He locks in the four-wheel drive. No streetlights out here, almost no neighbors. The place he chose.

The front tires carving snow, veering on a narrow path, close to an edge that falls not far but far enough to get stuck, about ten feet down to a meadow and stream. The truck would roll and he'd be trapped and it would be only an accident. But the problem is time. It would take hours to freeze or suffocate, longer if the truck was still running with its heater, and he might be rescued.

He climbs along the hill, knowing the road more from memory than sight. Trees still without leaves, white trunks and arms so thin. He reaches his own driveway, finally, up another slight hill, and his house is there, two story and empty, with a basketball hoop mounted, some dream of playing here with his son, but his son isn't coming, and most the year there's snow anyway.

He hits the garage door opener and it dutifully rises and he's inside, bare space brightly lit. Workbenches with only a few tools, a few boxes of his stuff not unpacked yet. Three sets of cross-country skis leaning in the corner, Tracy's pair so small. Fishing rods and nets. The zodiac parked on its trailer, tubes deflated, waiting for summer.

The concrete so clean, unstained. He lets himself in the kitchen door and puts his valise down on the folding card table. The place where the magnum will eventually be, so it might as well be there now. Economy of movement. Some efficiency at the end.

He's hungry, should have ordered food in the saloon. So it will be canned goods now, soup or chili. He opens the cabinets and stares at the choices, unable to decide. Bright labels and all unwanted. He decides finally on the chili, gets out a small pot and opens the can, so much like dog food, and waits for it to heat.

There's no stereo, no TV. No couch, no comfortable chairs. Nothing hanging on any wall. No one living here. Only a kitchen that extends to the wide-open living room with a fireplace at the other end, made of green stone he brought from the ranch in California, a reminder of home. Upstairs three bedrooms, all empty, and their bathrooms and a hallway. A place that can make sense only if it's filled.

He doesn't want to wash a bowl, so he brings the pot to the table and puts it on an oven glove and eats directly. A bit spicy, and hunks of meat, steaming in the cold, not bad. Pulls the magnum out of the valise and sets the valise on the floor, reaches down for the box of shells. He slides this open on the table in front of the pot, the fat copper casings lodged in Styrofoam, .44 REM MAG stamped on each ring outside the firing pin. Beautiful in their arrangement, and he pulls one out to look at it. The impossible weight of something so small. He can never get over how blunt the end, not coming to a point as rifle slugs do. This one is meant to tear and tumble and not go through easily at all. The plate of his skull will be smashed, not drilled.

He gets up to bring the phone over from the counter. A long enough cord to reach the table. Lifts the handset and starts to dial, then puts it back. He's not sure what to say.

He finishes the chili quickly, wonders if he should have another can. But that seems like too much work. So late and completely silent here, and the house freezing. He's still wearing his parka and gloves, waiting for the heating to do its job.

He's too tired to do it tonight. That's the truth. And it's not like there's any rush. Who cares whether he does it today or tomorrow? She might be asleep already anyway. He doesn't want to hear Rich in the background. He'll catch her tomorrow.

He finds a bag of chips and some peanuts and finishes his dinner with those. The brown vinyl of the card table, thin but slightly puffy, some sort of padding beneath. He sets the magnum perfectly in the center, as if mounted on display. Long barrel, and the grip looks stubby because everything else is so large, the enormous cylinder.

His head hurts so much in the cold. Unbearable to just sit here. So he walks upstairs to his bedroom and grabs codeine from behind the bathroom mirror and has two. Not something he can do all year or even all month, but he no longer has to worry about long-term effects. He should have tried all the recreational drugs. So many things he should have done.

He takes off his boots and parka, lies down in a big army surplus sleeping bag on the floor with an old pillow from hunting. Wears a beanie and also pulls the sleeping bag over his head, smelling his sour breath in close. All he can do is moan, the painkillers not kicking in yet.

He sees his thoughts begin, just setting out on another night of insomnia, one of thousands of nights like this, his body so exhausted and as soon as he rests his mind starts up. It's a small building, concrete, with a low ceiling, and the long line of thoughts that have been waiting outside patiently begin shuffling in. There's no room for them but they keep coming. That line is endless, and there are no rules about pressure, no limits. A thousand can pack into a space that should hold ten, and then a thousand more.

No clear connections, only crowding. Rhoda, mostly, desperate plans and regrets that still sting. Moments of decision. This last day not his first time seeing prostitutes. In such denial he could almost believe the ones in San Francisco were the first, but there were several here in Fairbanks, including the one that gave him crabs right before he visited Rhoda.

Trying to lie to her, making up some story about the locker room bench, and of course she wasn't fooled. Only his kids were fooled. But the moments when he took steps forward, calling the prostitute for instance. Why there was nothing to hold him back.

And the best moments with Rhoda, why there was nothing to make that remain. The summer in Gold Beach when they were building the boat, renovating a small house and working hard, always tired, but happy, too, dreaming of something together, fixing deviled ham sandwiches at the crappy little kitchen counter and playing grab ass. Sleeping on the floor then, too, in the same sleeping bag but too hot for summer, always throwing it off and sleeping naked wrapped around each other, the closest he's ever been to anyone. Her daughter, Cinamon, down in California with the grandparents, so he had Rhoda all to himself.

His kids visited later, but only part of the summer, David making coffee at the yard and getting hooked on caffeine, which Elizabeth was not happy about. Ten years old and a caffeine junkie, with about ten spoons of sugar in every cup. Tracy only five then and stayed for only a week, but he took walks with her, held her hand, and she was always saying she loved him, so easy and full.

A summer he only wanted to get through at the time, the construction late and fishing season passing, but if he could go back he would make it last longer, extend that summer a few extra months, because maybe that was the last time he felt hope.

After the launch, it was all struggle at sea, the boat sabotaged with small holes drilled through the fish holds, so the fish never froze and earned only half price. Then the drum crumpling in the Aleutians and having to sell and go back to dentistry. It wasn't all the struggle and disasters at sea but the return to dentistry, the return to the life he didn't want. That was when the end began, and all the moments between now and then might as well be erased.

His former lives: a kid in the water, in the lake, then old enough to hunt, the ranch and bucks and birds, then high school and dating, college and meeting Elizabeth, dental school and the navy in Alaska and having a son, being a dentist in Ketchikan and cheating when Elizabeth was pregnant with Tracy, living in California separate from his kids, then the commercial fishing and Alaska again, Fairbanks this time, and how does one map onto the other? So different, each life. They can't speak to each other. Even the times living in Alaska, each so different.

He doesn't want this set of lives. He wants a new set. So tired of going over everything. Regret is finally boredom as much as anything else. If he could erase his memories, he would. And maybe that's what he's doing, maybe that's the point of suicide.

He still doesn't believe he'll do it. That's a fact. No matter how many times he holds that pistol, he doesn't believe he'll actually pull the trigger.

The sound of the heating, the air getting warmer, and the refrigerator coming on. No other sounds. No neighbors, no cars that would pass here, no animals at this time of year, everything hidden away. No wind even. All still. The only movement is the pain in his head, spiral after spiral, deadened a bit by the codeine and accompanied now by that pukey, sweaty feeling of the drugs. Some hollow disbelief at the lack of sleep, even after so many nights. And he's too tired to get up and do anything. So he lies here a kind of waking mummy wrapped in despair. He weeps and weeps and his whole body hurts and the crying just will never end.

Sleep never does come. He has to rise several times to pee and drink, he blows his nose a hundred times, and he eats a bowl of cereal twice. The light finally comes in white and dark from clouds, just light without direction. Hard to know when sunrise is, but by the time the clock says six fifteen it must be there somewhere behind the cloud cover. He takes more codeine and has more cereal and lies down again to weep until seven thirty, which is eight thirty in California. He rises still dressed in Gary's clothes from the day before yesterday, too tired to change or maybe wanting to be in his brother's clothes, and he sits at the card table, at the one place possible, and picks up the phone receiver.

He dials information, asks for a flower shop in Lakeport, California, orders a dozen roses for Rhoda, for her birthday three days from now, to be delivered.

He picks up the magnum and puts it in his lap, just holds it for a while, feels his life moving, opens the cylinder and reaches for each slug in the Styrofoam and loads until the cylinder is full then snaps it shut. He places the pistol on the table by the phone, and he pulls back the hammer, makes sure the safety is off. Hair trigger, only one light touch now. He keeps his hands away.

He rises to get paper and pen, wants to write a note. He can't do this without a note, without some statement.

No paper in the kitchen but he goes upstairs and rummages through boxes in one of the spare bedrooms. Goose calls and his navy dress uniform. He still has the sword, ceremonial but also real, in its gold braid. All strange, from someone else's life. He never believed he was in the navy even when he was there. Their unit a joke anyway. The dentist leading them, marching backward, tripped and fell into a sandbox during one of the ceremonies. No one expected anything more from dentists.

That must have been one of the only days on Adak when the wind was low enough for them to be outside. Most of their time spent indoors and in tunnels. Hunting with the .300 magnum whenever the weather did clear. Shooting seals and sea lions and then trying to recover the bodies with a halibut gaff. Risking his life on the rocks, so slippery. Waves and thick green kelp. The water so cold and the hide rough.

Elizabeth almost blew away once. Went outside stupidly when the winds were over a hundred. So easy to die there, and yet no one did. Their friend run over by a bull sea lion, a thousand pounds, but mashed into the mud and nothing broken. David with jaundice at 105 degrees, almost dying right after birth but lived. Only the heart attacks died. The place didn't kill anyone, as dangerous as it was.

He finds a pen set given to him and has no memory when or from whom. Finds a large white pad of notepaper in a box of books, mostly westerns, and some old letters, including one he wrote to his uncle Frank in 1951, when he was ten.

Dear Uncle Frank: I have found the best place in the world to trap skunks. It is very high, and you have to crawl through a hole to get to it. There are many acorns, and it is very dark. I caught two civet cats there, and is very dangerous. I bet you wouldn't guess where it is.

I have had good luck in fishing this year. I have caught lots of catfish, and there are many worms. I caught about the biggest mudcat you ever saw in freshwater lakes, except in Lake Michigan, Superior, Erie, and Ontario. We gave two catfish to Mr. Lewis. The lake is up very high but it is going down.

I hope you can come up this summer. It is a lot of fun to ride on our launch. I will send you a funny story about some eager beavers. Ho yes do you know what a skunk is? A skunk is a pussycat with a fluid drive.

I forgot to tell you the danger about trapping skunks. The skunk might squirt you.

I forgot to tell you where I caught the skunks. Guess again.

Love, Jimmy

Jim reads the letter again, a way to touch that time, that different mind, not yet broken. Or were there signs even then? The dark place, the threat, the fascination with the fluid drive? Are we ever innocent? He should read these other letters, all of them, but he feels exhausted. He takes only the pad of paper and pen and returns downstairs.

Right now staying alive is only concern, he writes, as if it might be something to remember. Somehow he imagined a kind of letter might spring forth, but now he can tell this isn't going to happen. Nothing as simple as hunting or fishing to report. You shafted me, he writes. A note for Rhoda. What else does a suicide note contain? Who gets what, as in a will? There won't be anything after the IRS.

He writes his brother's name and phone number, Elizabeth also, and his father. *Please cremate my body in Fairbanks and scatter ashes at White Ranch.*

He gets his checkbook and writes checks to Gary, emptying most of that account.

Checks belong to Gary Vann. Choker belongs to Rhoda Vann. He's been carrying the choker around for a while now, a small gold chain, a piece of her, pulls it from his pocket and leaves it on the card table.

Gary—would like you to have White Ranch and hold one half in trust for David and Tracy.

Gary, you and all the relatives did everything you could possibly do. It's just that I need something that you can't give me.

Most scary thing is not being able to love again and not being able to maintain a relationship that would provide a fulfilling life for me.

He sets the pen down, holds his head in his hands, wishes the pain would just stop. But it's not enough. He can see that now. Nothing will ever be enough to make him do it. He's only going to play at suicide and write stupid notes that mean nothing. There will never be a time bad enough that it becomes inevitable. He picks up the pistol and holds the barrel to the side of his head. It should be like this, but accompanied by some crisis of spirit and memory and physical pain, something irresistible, something no one would be able to endure. And that is never going to happen. What he will be offered is much thinner than that.

He puts the pistol down, keeps it pointed carefully to the side in case it goes off, that hammer still pulled back, and reaches for the phone, dials Rhoda.

Waiting as the connections are found, a line snaking down to the doctor's office in Lakeport where she works now. This is how he could have found her in Lakeport. So stupid and easy and somehow he didn't think of it.

Someone else answers, so he has to ask for Rhoda, then wait again. They sound busy.

"Hello Jim," she finally says.

"I love you but I can't live without you," he says, a line he remembers now, already planned, and he picks up the pistol and places the barrel to the side of his head to make this more real. Phone receiver on the left, barrel on the right, like some kind of operator.

"What?" she asks. "I can't hear well. Hold on a minute."

He waits while there are scuffling sounds, and a door closing, and less background noise.

"Okay," she says. "I should be able to hear now."

"I love you but I'm not going to live without you," he says, and he feels none of the drama he had imagined, feels nothing in fact, and he knows he won't do it, won't pull the trigger, and then he does.

Acknowledgments

My stepmother, now named Nettie Rose, has always helped me in understanding my father. My gratitude to her for generosity, patience, and strength.

I also want to thank John L'Heureux, as always, for thirty years of mentorship and inspiration.

My thanks to Elisabeth Schmitz and Katie Raissian and others at Grove for their faith in my work, and of course to my perfect agents, Kim Witherspoon, David Forrer, Lyndsey Blessing, Rob Kraitt, and many others they work with. Thank you all for giving my books a life.

And to my family and to Nettie's family, an apology, with the thin excuse that I can't seem to do anything else.